OVER
35
STORIES
IN 1

GIANT
TREASURY
FOR **5** YEAR OLDS

Written by Pat Posner, Deborah Chancellor,
Liz Holliday, Ann Harth, Jillian Harker, Nick Ellsworth,
Jan Payne, Nicola Baxter, Tony Payne

Illustrated by Michelle Mathers, Martin Remphry,
Diana Catchpole

First published by Parragon in 2010

Parragon
Queen Street House
4 Queen Street
Bath BA1 1HE, UK

ISBN 978-1-4454-1112-5

Printed in Canada.

OVER
35
STORIES
IN 1

GIANT
TREASURY
FOR **5** YEAR OLDS

PaRragon

Bath · New York · Singapore · Hong Kong · Cologne · Delhi · Melbourne

Contents

The Science Project

Jed's mom was on the phone. Jed sat at the top of the stairs, listening carefully. "Mission understood, sir," said Mom. "You can rely on me." She put down the phone and went into the kitchen to finish making dinner.
Jed crept into Mom's office. She had left her work on the computer screen.

It told him all about her new mission. Jed smiled.

"Looks like we're going to be busy," he said quietly.

Mom tried to keep her job a secret from Jed, but he knew she was a special agent. A spy!

She worked for Unit X, a top-secret organization used by the government to sort out its trickiest problems.

Jed had a secret of his own: he sometimes helped Mom on her missions. But he made sure she never found out. Jed stared at the computer. An important new invention had disappeared: a new energy-saving fuel. Mom 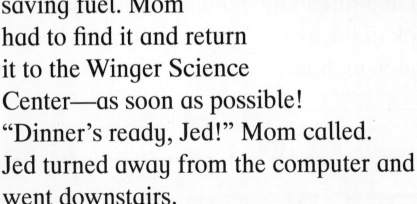 had to find it and return it to the Winger Science Center—as soon as possible!

"Dinner's ready, Jed!" Mom called. Jed turned away from the computer and went downstairs.

Mom gave him a plate of fried chicken and mashed potatoes. "Do you have any homework this weekend?" she asked.

Suddenly, Jed had an idea. "I have a science project on pollution," he replied. "My teacher said the Winger Science Center has a good exhibition. Can we go there, please?" Jed held his breath. Would Mom take the bait?

Mom looked surprised. "What a coincidence!" she said. "I have to visit the Winger Science Center tomorrow afternoon. You can come with me."

The next afternoon, Mom pulled into the Winger Science Center parking lot. "I'll go and talk to the manager while you look at the exhibition," she said. "Meet you in an hour."

Car Park

"OK," Jed replied. But as Mom walked away, Jed ran off around the side of the building.

Seeing an open window on the ground floor, Jed climbed through it. He found himself in a long hallway. Suddenly he heard a familiar voice. Mom!

Jed quickly hid behind a big plant as Mom turned the corner, talking to the research center manager.

"Here's my office," said the manager, opening a door.

Jed breathed a sigh of relief as they disappeared inside. Then Jed heard another voice.

"Here, Kitty!" it called, from a nearby room.

A large cat hurried past. Jed followed it to a boiler room, where an old janitor was putting cat food into a bowl. Jed watched from behind the door.

The cat rubbed up against the janitor, purring loudly.

The janitor chuckled. "You like

12

this food, don't you, Kitty?" he said, as
the cat began to eat. "But you don't like
that new kitty litter, do you?" he added.
He looked at a litter box on the floor.
"That stuff's useless!"
He wandered off, muttering, "And
whoever heard of PINK kitty litter!"
Jed went over to pet the kitty. He looked
at the kitty litter box as he passed.
Sure enough, it was full of bright-pink
pellets. How weird. Jed looked at the
label on the bag next to the tray.

This was no ordinary kitty litter—it was the missing fuel! Jed gave the cat a hurried pat, and then grabbed a 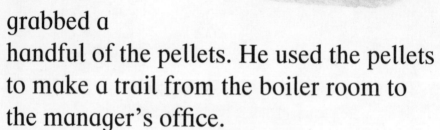 handful of the pellets. He used the pellets to make a trail from the boiler room to the manager's office.

He glanced at his watch. The hour was nearly up. "Time to go!" he said, running back to the exhibition.

A few minutes later, Jed's mom appeared. She was smiling.

"That was easier than I thought," she said. "Have you found what you wanted too, Jed?"

"Yes thanks, Mom!" Jed replied, smiling back at her.

Garage Sale

"Kayla! Kayla! We've got something to show you!"
Kayla sighed as Jordan and Tom, her two little brothers, barged into her bedroom. "I'm busy with my friends," she told them. "Show me later."

When the two little boys had gone Kayla
sighed again. "Sorry about that," she said
to Ava, Emily, and Mia. "They were just
being nosy."
"It's the same whoever's house we meet
in," said Emily. "Our brothers or sisters
always interrupt us."
"We need somewhere private to meet,"
said Mia thoughtfully, eating one of Kayla's chocolate cupcakes. "Kayla, your
cupcakes are delicious!"

There was a knock at the door. Kayla's dad called out, "I've brought you girls some juice!"

Kayla opened the door. "Thanks, Dad," she said.

"You all look a bit serious," said her dad. "Anything I can help with?"

"Not unless you can wave a magic wand and find a private place for the four of us to hang out," Kayla replied.

"Abracadabra! Spare garage."

17

Kayla almost dropped the tray. "Could we really use it, Dad?" she asked.

"It would help me, too," her dad said. "Your mom's been on my case for a while to clear it out. You'll have to do that if you want to use it."

After they'd had their snack, the girls hurried out to the garage.

"It's kind of gloomy," Kayla said. "We'll have to paint it."

"We need to get rid of all this trash first," said Ava.

"It isn't all trash," Kayla protested. "This pail has got a hole in it, but my grandma uses things like this for growing plants."

Ava held up a pair of boots. "One's got a broken zipper," she said. "I bet someone could fix it. There's nothing wrong with the other boot."

"I know, we'll have a garage sale!" said Emily. "We can use the money we make to buy paint."

"I think you should make some of your cupcakes for us to sell too, Kayla," said Mia. "They're great!"

"I'll start baking!" laughed Kayla.

The girls decided to hold the sale the next day. "We'll have it at the front of the house," Kayla said. "We can put everything on Dad's work table."
But nobody spent as much as the girls had hoped. The only thing everyone really wanted to buy were Kayla's chocolate cupcakes.
Back in the garage, Ava sat on a wooden bench and counted the money. "It only comes to $6.65," she told them with a sigh. "And at least $5.00 of that came

from Kayla's cupcakes!"

"It must be more than that!" Kayla said. "Move over! I'll count it again."

Ava shuffled along the bench. Then the bench tilted upwards and Ava yelled as she slid to the floor.

Kayla yelled too, when she saw that the bench had been resting across two large cans of paint. "It's yellow," she said, reading the label. "Just what we need. I'll run and ask Dad if we can have it."

"Don't mind me," said Ava. "I'll just stay here on the floor."

21

When Kayla returned, she was smiling. "Yes!" she said. "We can have the paint."

"And $6.65 should be enough to buy some paintbrushes," said Ava. "Thanks to Kayla's cupcakes!"

"There's only one thing left to decide," said Emily. "Now that we've got a clubhouse, we need a club name."

"Isn't it obvious?" said Ava.

"No," said Mia and Kayla together.

"The Cupcake Club!" said Ava.

London Lesson

It was the first day of the summer vacation and Robbie, Laura, and Janie were busy packing. Their guitarist dad was going on a world tour with his band, and they were going with him and Mom! "Make sure you've packed your swimsuits *and* your warm sweaters," Mom called. "You never know what you might need."

"Taxi's here!" shouted Dad.

"Come on, Dad," said Robbie, when everyone had piled in. "Give us a clue where we're going first."

Dad grinned. "OK," he said. "It's a capital city."

"Rome!" shouted Laura.

"Washington!" said Robbie.

"Dublin!" Janie suggested.

"No, no, and no," answered Mom.

"Here's another clue... Buckingham Palace."

"London!" Robbie, Laura, and Janie shouted together.

"That's right," Dad said. "Our first stop is London."

On the way to London in the plane, Mom had another surprise for them. "I'm going to give you all a challenge in each place we stop," she said. "If you complete them all, there will be an extra-special treat at the end of the trip."

Robbie cheered. "Easy!" he said. "Everyone loves Dad—as soon as they see him they'll help us with our tasks."

"Not so fast!" said Dad. "That would be too easy. Besides, I'll be rehearsing with the band most of the time. You'll have to do this by yourselves."

There was a huge crowd of fans and newspaper reporters waiting for Dad and the other band members when they landed in London. Dad talked to them for a little while and signed autographs before they went to their hotel.

Once they had settled into their room, Mom announced the first challenge to them. "I'd like a photo showing *all* of London!" she said.

"We need to find somewhere really high up," said Janie, switching on her laptop. A few minutes later, she looked up. "I think we should take a ride on the London Eye. It's a giant Ferris wheel near the

River Thames," she suggested. "This site says that from the top of the wheel, you can see 25 miles in every direction!"

Next morning, Dad went to rehearse with the band while Mom took Laura, Robbie, and Janie to the riverside.

"There's the wheel!" shouted Robbie. The huge wheel, with its metal spokes and thirty-two glass passenger pods, rose up above the buildings into the sky.

"This is going to be great!" said Laura, when it was their turn to step into a giant glass pod.

"Look!" Mom pointed across the river as the pod moved upwards. "There are the

Houses of Parliament and Big Ben."
She turned. "And look over there.
There's Buckingham Palace, where the
Queen lives!"
"I don't know which way to point the
camera," Janie complained. "Whichever
way I face, I'm going to leave lots of
London out of the picture!"
Too soon, it was time to leave London.

"The views of London were amazing," said Robbie in the taxi to the airport. "But we've failed our very first challenge. Now we won't get our special treat at the end of the tour."

Just after the plane took off, Laura looked out of the window. "Quick, Janie!" she yelled excitedly. "Give me the camera!"

Janie quickly pulled the camera out of her bag and handed it over.

Laura held the camera up to the window and took a picture.

"Look down there," she told the others with a grin. "All of London!"
"Good job!" said Mom. "I knew you could do it."

Dragon Danger

"Look what I found in the attic." Joe's mom came into his bedroom, carrying a dusty old book. "I think it might have belonged to Grandpa when he was a boy," she said, handing it to Joe. She hurried out to continue her organizing for tomorrow's garage sale.

Joe turned away from his computer to look at the book.

On the first page was a picture of a castle. He looked at it closely. It seemed almost real. Suddenly Joe felt dizzy. "I must have been playing computer games for too long," he thought. He closed his eyes for a second—but when he opened them, he wasn't in his bedroom any more. He was falling quickly through fluffy white clouds… until he landed with a bump.

"Duck!" shouted a squeaky voice.
Joe ducked. An arrow whizzed past.
"Where am I?" Joe asked. "What's that terrible roaring noise?"
"You don't know much, do you?" said the squeaky voice. "You're on the roof of Neeve Castle. We're under attack—and that's the roar of the enemy's dragon!"

Joe looked down. A tiny green sprite stared up at him—about a foot tall, with pointed ears.

"Um, did you say *dragon*?" he said, peering over the parapet. There was a huge, terrifying shape among the soldiers firing at the castle. "And how on earth did I get here?"

"No idea," said the sprite cheerfully. "I'm Chee, by the way. Can you put me on your shoulder, so that I can see what's going on?"

Just then, a hail of sharp arrows came
flying toward Joe and Chee.
"Aaargh!" cried Joe. He ducked,
toppled… and the two of them fell from
the castle wall and *splash!* into the
castle moat. Before he knew what was
happening, a hand had scooped Joe out
of the water, gasping and spluttering.
"I've taken a prisoner!" shouted an
enemy soldier triumphantly.

Then he began to yell, "Ouch!" and let go. Chee was kicking the soldier's ankles! "Run for it!" shouted the sprite. Joe scooped Chee up and ran as fast as he could away from the castle. But before they got far, a great shadow fell over them. It was the dragon's wing.

Chee jumped down. "Please don't hurt us," he said, in a very small voice.

The dragon spoke softly but deeply. "I do not want to hurt you," it said. Joe realized that the creature wore a muzzle and that its wings were chained together.

"King Barzan had me muzzled and chained," continued the dragon. "But if you free me, I will help you."

"Don't listen. It's a trick!" cried Chee.
Joe looked over his shoulder. Five enemy
soldiers were running toward him. Then
he looked at the dragon.

Its face was fierce, but its eyes seemed
friendly.

"We don't have a lot of choice, Chee!" he
said with a gulp, and quickly unchained
the dragon.

With a great flapping, the dragon soared
into the sky. It swooped around and
chased the enemy soldiers away, snorting
flames of fire.

King Sten and Queen Talia, rulers of
Neeve, thanked the dragon, Joe, and
Chee for saving them.

"And now can you send me home,
please?" said Joe, hopefully.

"I'm sorry, Joe, but I don't have that
power," said the King with a sigh. "I
believe there is a magical link between
your world and ours. Many years ago I
visited your world, through a picture like
you have. But I feared others might fall
through it and never come back, so I tore
the picture up and gave the three pieces
to my old teacher, Mistress Swift, for
safekeeping."

"I'll have to find Mistress Swift, then,"
said Joe. "Or I'll never get home!"

"I know the way to Mistress Swift's tower. I shall show you!" Chee told him. "Take this horn," said the dragon. "It is made from my claw, and if you are in need blow it and I shall hear—but be warned, it will work only once."
Joe suddenly missed his home very much. "Come on, Chee," he said with a sigh. "I suppose it isn't far to Mistress Swift's. I might even be home in time for dinner!"

Basketball: Short Shooter

Coach Travers clapped her hands. "We have two new students today," she said. "Daniel? Sophie? Come up here, please."
Daniel and his sister walked under the basketball hoop and across the wooden floor. They stood beside Coach Travers

and looked at their new classmates. The class stared back.

"This is Daniel and Sophie Lutz," Coach Travers said. "They're twins."

Coach Travers turned to Sophie.

"We have a few teams at Park Street Elementary School, Sophie. What's your favorite sport?"

"Soccer," Sophie said right away.

A couple of girls in the front row smiled and gave her a thumbs-up sign.

"And how about you, Daniel?" Coach Travers asked.

Daniel held his breath. He looked at the hoop above his head. He'd give anything to play on the school team.

"I like basketball," he mumbled.

Coach Travers nodded, but quiet laughter and whispers came from some of the class.

"You're too short for basketball!" a boy called.

Daniel's face felt hot.

"He's not!" Sophie said, defending her brother. "He practices with our big brother Mark all the time!"

Coach Travers turned to the boy who'd called out. "Get the basketballs, please,

Jason," she said. "We're playing basketball today."

The familiar sound of bouncing balls made Daniel feel calm. He stood in line with the others, shooting at the basket when it was his turn. Balls escaped into every corner of the room, but Daniel never missed a shot.

Coach Travers blew a whistle. "Jason and Daniel, come here please."

The two boys stood beside each other in front of the coach. Daniel was a lot  shorter than Jason. "I've been watching you, Daniel," Coach Travers said. "I need another player for the basketball team." She bounced the ball to him. "If you can get a basket past Jason, then you're on the team."

Jason laughed. "Ready, shorty?" he said. He spread his arms.

The class was silent as Daniel stood on his toes to peer over the taller boy's shoulder. The basket looked far away. He took a deep breath.

"If you can beat Mark, you can beat Jason!" Sophie yelled.

Jason waved his arms. "Come on, shorty, move!"

Daniel did.

He dribbled the ball and ducked under
Jason's arm. He raced toward the
basket, but Jason jumped in front of him.
Keeping his body between Jason and the
ball, Daniel turned his back on the taller
boy. He sped away from the basket.
His mind moved faster than his feet as
Daniel worked out a plan. Mark had

taught him a new move. It just might work. Could he do it?

As he reached center court, Daniel slowed. The footsteps behind him grew faster and closer. When it sounded like Jason was in a full sprint, Daniel stepped to the side and spun around. He raced toward his basket.

"Hey!" Jason shouted from behind.
Daniel threw the ball as Jason skidded to
a stop. They both watched the ball sail
toward the net. It hit the rim once, twice,
and then a third time before it dropped
through the hoop and hit the floor.
"Do you still think he's too short, Jason?"
someone yelled.
Jason picked up the ball and handed it to
Daniel. "Welcome to the team," he said
with a smile.

The Royal Mystery

"Jed, go and clean your room!" shouted Mom. She was in a bad mood.
"But it is clean!" Jed protested, stomping upstairs. "Maybe she's having trouble with a mission," he said to himself. "I'd better check what she's up to."
While Mom was in the shower, Jed took a look at her computer screen.

"The Duchess of Muddleswick has been disappearing from her house every night," he read. "The government thinks she may be working as a spy. Your mission is to find out what she is doing." Jed went back to his bedroom. He would follow Mom to work that evening.

Jed put a pillow under his blanket to make Ann, the babysitter, think he was asleep if she looked in on him. Then he turned out the light, opened his window and climbed out. He hid in the shadows, waiting for Mom to leave the house.

A few moments later, Mom came out and began to walk down the street.

Jed followed her. After a short bus ride
and a long walk, she stopped outside a
huge house.

"That must be the Duchess's mansion,"
Jed said to himself.

Mom's cell phone rang. As she talked on
the phone, she didn't notice a shadowy
figure quickly leave the house through a
side door.

Jed watched. It was a woman wearing sunglasses—even though it was dark. Jed guessed it must be the Duchess.

Jed left his mom talking and followed the Duchess down a half-hidden little alley. At the end of it was another street with lots of stores and restaurants.

Jed watched as the Duchess slipped into Jimmy's Diner. He followed her in.

"What will you have tonight, my dear?" the man behind the counter asked.

"My favorite: burger and fries, please, Jimmy!" said the Duchess, cheerfully. "It's such a shame that they never serve it at the banquets I go to. That's why I come here!"

Smiling, Jed slipped out of the restaurant and went home.

The next evening was Mom's night off. "Can we go out to eat tonight?" Jed asked her.

Mom sighed. "I don't feel like cooking, so that's fine by me," she said gloomily. "I want a burger and fries," said Jed. "And I heard about a really great place in town. It's called Jimmy's Diner."

At Jimmy's, Jed and Mom sat down to eat their burgers.
A few minutes later, in walked the Duchess. Mom nearly choked on a fry.

"Hello, my dear. How nice to see you again!" said Jimmy.
"I just can't keep away from your delicious food, Jimmy," said the Duchess with a smile.

"Now let me think—I'll have my usual
burger and fries, please!"
Jed's mom smiled for the first time in
days. "I'm glad we went out to eat, Jed,"
she said. "This was a great place
to come!"
Jed nodded. Another mystery solved!

In the Swim

"Earth calling Kayla! Come in Kayla!" called Mia.

Ava and Emily giggled.

"Sorry, what did you say?" Kayla asked. "I was thinking."

"What about?" Mia demanded.

"We had a mail from the animal shelter this morning," Kayla replied.

"The one we got Bouncer from. They're trying to raise money to build a new kennel."

"You want us to do something to help," guessed Emily.

Kayla nodded.

"Well... we're no good at selling stuff," said Ava with a grin. "We only made $6.65 when we had our garage sale!"

Emily chewed her thumb, thinking hard.

"Got it!" she yelled. "What did we all get a trophy for?"

"Swimming?" Mia asked.

"Swimming," Emily agreed. "We could do a sponsored swim. I'm sure our moms would let us."

The girls decided to go and ask them right away.

All the moms agreed.

"But how will you get people to sponsor you?" Mia's dad asked. "You can't go around knocking on doors."

"I know!" said Mia. "Mom, will you call the supermarket manager and ask him if we could stand in the supermarket entrance?" Mia's mom worked part-time at the local supermarket. The four friends looked hopefully at her.

"All right," Mia's mom agreed. "I'll do it now."

The girls waited impatiently.

When she got off the phone, Mia's mom

smiled at the Cupcake Club and gave a thumbs-up sign.

The girls yelled their thanks, and then hurried back to the clubhouse to make plans.

"We won't be going inside the supermarket," said Kayla. "Let's take Bouncer and Emily's dog Sheba with us."

Emily nodded. "Excellent idea. We could put water wings on their legs."

The friends spent the rest of the afternoon making a large poster and some sponsorship sheets.

The following morning, Mia's mom drove the girls and the two dogs down to the supermarket.

She showed them where to stand. "I'll be at the checkout, number eight," she said. "So I'll be able to keep an eye on you."

Mia and Ava put the poster on the wall next to the supermarket entrance. Emily and Kayla fixed the water wings onto their dogs.

A lot of people stopped to look and smile, but only one or two offered sponsorship.

"I'm fed up," Ava said after a couple of hours. "Hardly anyone is sponsoring us." Just then, a man and a woman ran out of the store.

"Come on, hurry!" yelled the man. Bouncer and Sheba jumped around in excitement.

The woman fell over Bouncer and everything in her shopping bag fell out.

She knocked into the man and he fell over, too.
Suddenly, a security guard ran out of the store. "Stop, thief!" he shouted.
He grabbed the man and woman and

marched them back inside, along with the shopping bag.

The girls tried to calm down Bouncer and Sheba, talking excitedly.

"They must have been shoplifters," said Emily curiously.

Soon afterward, the supermarket manager came out to the girls. "Thank you!" he said. "Your dogs stopped those shoplifters from getting away. I think you all deserve a reward."

"Will you sponsor our swim?" Mia asked immediately.

The manager grinned. "I was going to suggest $2.00 for every lap," he said.

"Wow!" the friends said together.

"Did you hear that, Bouncer?" said Kayla, hugging her dog.

"We'll swim more laps than we ever have before!" said Emily.

"You bet we will!" Ava agreed.

Paris Prize

Next stop was Paris, France. While Dad was with the band, getting ready for that evening's concert, Mom took Laura, Robbie, and Janie sightseeing.
First they went to see the Eiffel Tower. Then they walked along the Left Bank of the River Seine, past all the artists who were painting there.

"When are you going to give us our next challenge, Mom?" Laura asked.

"Soon," Mom said. "Ah, here we are..."

They'd stopped outside a riverside cafe. "I came here with Dad a long time ago," Mom told them, leading them inside. "I've never forgotten the delicious chocolate mousse I had here. Your challenge is to get the recipe."

"Well, this challenge should be easy," said Janie, as they were shown to a table. But Mom explained that she had asked the chef for the recipe before and he'd said it was a secret.

At the next table, a woman was talking to the waiter. "The chocolate mousse was simply delicious!" she exclaimed. "I really must have the recipe."

"I am sorry, madam," said the waiter. "That is impossible."

"I'm willing to pay for it," the lady

64

persisted. She gave him a big smile.
The waiter shook his head. "Many people
have offered to buy the recipe," he said
snootily. "Our chef always says no."
The lady sighed. Then she got up and left
the cafe.
"We're never going to get the recipe!"

whispered Laura, as the waiter came over
to take their order.

"Yes we are," Robbie whispered back.
"I've got an idea. Wait and see."

He turned to the waiter. "Soup, please!"

The waiter came back with their orders.
As he put down Robbie's soup, Robbie
turned and nudged the waiter's arm.

SPLOOSH!

Pea soup spilled all down Robbie's
tee shirt.

"Oh, I'm so sorry!" said the waiter. He started to dab at Robbie's tee shirt with a napkin.

"Oh no!" Robbie cried. "My tee shirt might be ruined, and it's my favorite!"

"Come with me to the kitchen. I'll wash the soup off," the waiter said. As Robbie followed the waiter, he turned and winked at the others.

Watching over a team of cooks in the kitchen was a huge man in a tall chef's hat.

"I'm really sorry, Chef," said the waiter, "but I spilled pea soup all over this young customer."

"It's my favorite tee shirt," Robbie explained, as he took it off and handed it to the waiter.

The chef turned to Robbie. "I'm very sorry. Perhaps some of my special chocolate mousse while you're waiting?" Robbie nodded eagerly.

He took a mouthful. "It's very good," he agreed. "But my mom's apple pie is better. She uses a secret recipe my grandma gave her."

The chef went bright red. "I must
learn how to make this wonderful apple
pie that is better than my mousse!"
he exclaimed.
"Oh, I don't think Mom would tell you.
It's a family secret," said Robbie.
The chef looked like he might start
crying.
The waiter came back with Robbie's tee
shirt. "Well," Robbie said thoughtfully,
as he put it back on. "Perhaps Mom
would swap her apple pie recipe for your
mousse recipe. I could ask..."

"Please do!" said the chef. He went to a drawer and took out a piece of paper. "Here is my recipe. Now, go quickly and ask your mother!"

Clutching the recipe, Robbie hurried out to the others.

"Good job," said Mom, writing her apple pie recipe down on a napkin. "Just don't tell Grandma!"

Mistress Swift's Tower

"Why is King Barzan at war with King Sten?" Joe asked on the way to Mistress Swift's tower.

Chee sighed. "Nine moons ago, King Barzan asked for Princess Talia's hand in marriage," he explained. "But Princess Talia married King Sten instead, and

became the new Queen of Neeve.
King Barzan was so angry, he swore he
would destroy them both."
Joe shivered. King Barzan sounded like a
fearsome enemy.
By the time Joe and Chee arrived at
Mistress Swift's tower, it was nearly dark
and the moon was rising. Joe knocked
on the door. There was no reply, so he
knocked again, as hard as he could.

An old lady popped her head out of a high window. "Go away!" she shouted. "It's too late for visitors!"

"But King Sten sent us, Mistress Swift!" Chee called up to her.

"Oh!" exclaimed Mistress Swift. "Then I suppose you'd better come up," she said. A few minutes later, the door to the tower opened and Mistress Swift let them in.

"Mistress Swift, I've come to seek your help," Joe told her. "I need you to give me the torn-up pieces of the magic picture you hid for the king."

Mistress Swift frowned. "I'm sorry, I can't remember where I put them," she said. "Goodbye!"

Joe gasped. "Oh no!" he cried. "Without them, I won't be able to go home. I'll be stuck here for ever!"

The old lady sighed. "I suppose I could have a quick look for the pieces of the picture," she said.

She wandered over to the couch and picked up a cushion. "No, they're not under there," she said. Then she picked up a teapot from the table. "No, not under there," she said.

"Mistress Swift isn't looking very hard," Joe whispered to Chee.

Chee shook his head. "This is very unlike Mistress Swift," he whispered back. Then, as Mistress Swift went to open the closet, Joe saw her reflection in a mirror hanging on the wall. It didn't look like her at all! In the mirror, Mistress Swift was thin and bony, with a pointed face and long teeth—just like the enemy soldiers.

"Look, Chee!" Joe cried, pointing to the reflection.

"Oh no!" gasped Chee.

"You'd better tell us what's going on, Mistress Swift!" said Joe.

"What have you done to the real Mistress Swift?" shouted Chee.

"I won't!" said the creature pretending to be Mistress Swift. "Do you think I'm scared of you? Now go away!"

"I'm going to call King Sten's dragon," said Joe. He quickly pulled out the dragon-claw horn.

Mistress Swift suddenly looked very

scared. "No!" she said. And then, without any warning, she started to change in front of Joe's eyes. In just seconds she had changed into a column of gray smoke that whirled out of the window, leaving nothing behind.

"What a lucky escape!" said Chee. "It must have been a shape-shifter! King Barzan uses them to spy on his enemies—and they're very dangerous. The only thing that can hurt them is dragon fire. No wonder it was scared when you threatened to call the dragon!"

Just then, Joe heard banging coming from the top of the tower.

"Help! Help!" a distant voice was crying. Joe and Chee raced up the spiral staircase, and found the real Mistress Swift locked in the very top room.

"I can't thank you enough for rescuing me from the shape-shifter," she said. "Now, how can I help you?"

Joe explained that he needed the three pieces of King Sten's picture so that he could go home.

"But the pieces aren't here," said Mistress Swift. "I gave one piece to the king's sister and one piece to each of his two brothers. They rule the furthest three corners of Neeve for him."

"Then I suppose I'll have to visit all three of them," sighed Joe. "This is turning out to be quite an adventure!"

Girls' Soccer: Teamwork

"Hey, Sophie! Ready for your first game?" called Amelia, captain of the Park Street Elementary School Girls' Soccer Team.

Sophie finished putting her shoes on and stood up. "I think so," she said. "What's the Oakfield Elementary team like?"

"They're one of the best," Amelia replied. "It's going to be a good game!" Sophie looked around. A lot of people had come to watch! Her stomach jumped and her palms felt damp.

"Hey! Sophie!" a voice called from the side.

Sophie spotted her brother. She smiled and waved. Just knowing Daniel was there made her feel better. She jogged onto the field and took her position.

"Let's go for it, Park Street!" called Amelia.

Coach Travers placed the ball on the center line and stood back. Park Street was kicking off first.

Amelia raced up to the ball and kicked it

to Jackie. The game was on!
The ball was a blur as it was dribbled
and passed from one girl to another.
Sophie forgot to be nervous as she played
the game she loved best.

"Julia!" Sophie passed the ball and
watched Julia shoot it past the goalie
and into the net. Coach Travers blew her
whistle. "Goal!" she shouted.

The first half of the game flew by. Sophie kicked, blocked, and defended. She was always in the right place to pass to the girl who scored.

By the end of the first half, Park Street Elementary was ahead by one goal. The score was 3-2.

Sophie waved to Daniel as she ran onto the field for the second half of the game. She was glad he was watching. She just wished she could score a goal. Then she'd really feel like a part of the team.

The game continued. Oakfield Elementary scored another goal so the score was an even 3-3. With only five minutes left in the game, it was Park Street's turn to kick off.

Sophie wiped her face and hands on her shirt. They needed one more goal. Could they do it?
Amelia kicked the ball and Julia raced after it. She was fast, but not fast enough! A forward from Oakfield stole the ball and dribbled down the field.

Sophie sprinted after the forward. Her feet pounded into the grass. The forward's ponytail swished just out of reach. Sophie pushed her legs harder. She edged past and touched the ball with her toe. It spun to the side where Julia was ready.

Julia dribbled the ball back toward the Oakfield goal. Sophie raced down the field after her.

"Sophie!" Julia passed the ball to Sophie. Sophie dribbled it for a few steps but wasn't close enough to make a shot. She looked for a teammate who was clear. "It's yours, Amelia!" Sophie kicked the ball toward the team captain and Amelia flicked it into the goal.

"Goal!" Coach Travers shouted. "Park Street wins!"

Sophie ran to help the team lift Amelia onto their shoulders. But then she stopped. The rest of the team were now running toward her!

"What are you doing?" Sophie asked, as the girls crowded around her, smiling.

"It takes more than one person to score a goal, Sophie," Amelia said, as she and the rest of the team lifted Sophie into the air. "You helped to score them all!"

The President's Secret

"I have to leave early today, Jed," said Mom, grabbing her keys. "See you later!" As the front door slammed shut, Jed switched on the TV. He didn't have to leave for school just yet.

He flicked onto the news channel.
"No one knows what is wrong with the
President," said a newscaster. A picture
of the President flashed up on the screen
behind him. "He hasn't been seen in
public for over a week now."

Jed yawned and then went into the study to get his book bag. As he passed the computer, he couldn't resist checking to see what Mom was up to today.

There was a photo of a bald man on the screen. He looked oddly familiar.

"The President's toupee disappeared last week," Jed read.

He looked at the photo again and his eyes widened. The man in the photo was the President, without his thick mop of gray hair. The President wore a toupee—and no one knew! Jed read on. "The President's dog chewed up his spare toupee, and a new toupee cannot be made since the President's hairdresser has broken his arm in a skiing accident. You must find the lost toupee as quickly as possible, Agent Best."

Jed grinned. "I'll have to think of a good excuse for being late for school today," he said.

Half an hour later, Jed was standing at the back of 1600 Pennsylvania Avenue, where the President lived. He checked that no one was looking and then quickly climbed the wall and dropped into the

garden. He sneaked up to the house, grinning when he saw that the back door had a dog flap.

Jed squeezed through it and found himself in a large kitchen.
"Is that you, Bruno?" said a woman's voice. The voice was now coming toward the kitchen.

Jed quickly ducked behind some
recycling bins.

"Woof woof!" A big, shaggy dog brushed
past him.

"Come on, time for breakfast, Bruno,"
said the woman.

Jed spotted a closet. "I'll wait in there
while she feeds the dog," he thought,
slipping inside.

It was a broom
closet. As his eyes
got used to the dark,
Jed spotted something
in the corner. "That's
a strange mop," he
thought.
He leaned down
to take a closer look.
It wasn't a mop at all.
"It's the missing toupee!" Jed whispered.
Someone had mistaken it for a mop head!
Jed shook the toupee and coughed as a
cloud of dust filled the closet.
When the kitchen was empty, Jed crept
out of the closet again, clutching the
toupee carefully.
He went to find the President's office.
When he found the right door, Jed hung
the scruffy toupee onto the door knob.
Then Jed gave the door two short knocks
and hid behind a nearby chair.

The door opened. Jed heard a gasp—and then saw a hand snatch up the toupee and slam the door shut again.

Jed smiled. "I guess it's time for school now," he said to himself.

That evening, Mom arrived home from work early, in a very good mood.

Jed was watching the news. "Look at the President!" he said. "He sure is having a bad hair day!"

Party Planners

It was Emily's brother's sixth birthday. Their dad had taken Daniel and his friends to see a movie. Afterward, they were having a birthday party back at the house. The best friends were helping to prepare the food.

"Two of you can make the rice krispie treats," said Emily's mom.

"We will!" Emily and Kayla volunteered.

"You'll need rice krispies, melted butter, and syrup," said Emily's mom. "I've melted the butter and mixed in the marshmallows for you." She pointed to a large bowl, next to a box of rice krispies and a baking sheet.

"Ava and Mia, would you spread this tray of cookies with chocolate frosting,

please?" Emily's mom asked.

"The frosting is in that big glass bowl."

"Yes!" Ava said, beaming happily.

"We have the best job!" said Mia. She and Ava did a high five.

Emily and Kayla laughed.
An hour later, most of the food
was ready. Emily's mom took a sponge
cake out of the oven and put it on the
kitchen table. "When that's cool we'll
put frosting in the middle, and then we're
done!" she said.
Just then, they heard a noise from the
baby monitor. Emily's mom looked at her
watch. "Noah's woken up from his nap.

He wants his dinner," she said. She went
to get Emily's youngest brother.
"I'll get Noah's high chair ready, Mom!"
Emily called after her. She carried the
high chair from the corner of the kitchen
and set it next to the kitchen table.
Emily's mom came in with a
still-sleepy Noah.
"He's so cute," said Kayla.
Noah was put into his high chair with a
couple of toys. Emily's mom got his food
out of the fridge.

"Would you like to feed him, Kayla?" she asked.

"Yes please!" Kayla said eagerly.

She pulled up a chair next to Noah and started spooning food into his mouth, pretending the spoon was an airplane.

Everyone laughed and Noah was so
excited he started banging his toys on the
high chair.
Suddenly, his arm flew out—and his toy
hammer came down thud in the middle
of the cooling sponge cake!
"Ooooh!" said Noah.

Emily started to giggle.
And then so did everyone else.
"Oh, dear," said her mom, wiping away
a tear of laughter with her apron.

"Anyone got any ideas for using cake crumbs?"

"I know!" said Mia. "My mom makes this great dessert. She mixes cake crumbs with chocolate frosting. Then she rolls it all up into balls and dips them in chocolate sprinkles. I helped her make them last Christmas."

Ava held up the glass bowl. "And there's still some chocolate frosting left to make them with!"

"Fantastic!" said Emily's mom. "But you'll have to work fast," she added, looking at her watch. "Daniel and his friends will be back in half an hour."

"Right," said Kayla. "Em, we can play with Noah in the living room while Ava and Mia make the dessert."

Emily nodded. "We'll take a frying pan," she said. "Noah loves banging on a frying pan with a wooden spoon."

Noah banged away happily while Emily and Kayla blew up balloons.

Half an hour later, Daniel and his friends arrived home from the movie.

"Wow!" they said.

All the birthday food was on the table in the living room and the balloons were pinned around the walls.

Everyone said it was the best birthday party ever!

Sydney Snap

Janie, Robbie, and Laura were very
excited when they discovered that next
they were going to Sydney, Australia.
"Can't you come out exploring with us,
Dad?" Laura asked, when they'd settled
into their hotel. "Just this once?"

"Sorry," said Dad. "I have to rehearse with the band, but you can tell me about it later."

It was very hot and sunny, so they had to use sunscreen and wear hats.

Mom took them for a walk around Sydney Harbor and past the Opera House, where Dad's band was playing that evening. The Opera House was famous because of its unusual shape.

"Isn't it beautiful?" Mom sighed.
"It looks like a pile of seashells," said Robbie.

"Mom?" Janie asked. "This is great, but shouldn't you tell us what our challenge is? Suppose we don't have time to do it before we leave!"

"Don't worry, you'll find out tomorrow," Mom said.

"We're going to a wildlife park," Mom said the next morning. "I'll tell you what your challenge is when we get there."

There was a car waiting for them outside the hotel. They all got in. Soon they were driving up into the hills.

"It's time for your challenge!" Mom told them when they reached the wildlife park.

"I want you to have your photo taken hugging a koala."

"Ooh, sounds fun!" Laura said. "I'm going to like this challenge!"

"This should be easy," said Robbie. They got into a yellow bus with some other tourists. A park ranger drove them around to look at the animals.

"If you look around you, you'll see wallabies and kangaroos," said the ranger. "And if you look in the trees you might see a bird called a kookaburra."

"What about the koalas?" Janie asked. "We have to see those!"

"Don't worry," said the ranger with a grin. "You'll see some koalas too."

The bus came to a place where they were

allowed to get out. Tall trees stretched high above them.

"The koalas are up there," said the ranger, pointing up in the trees.

It was very hard to see any koalas because they were so high up. Luckily Mom had some binoculars. They all took turns looking through them.

"Are there any tame koalas?" Laura asked. "We have to get our photo taken hugging one."

The ranger shook his head. "The koalas might look cuddly, but they're still wild animals," he warned. "And in any case, they're protected, which means we can't touch them."

"Oh no!" said Janie.

"How are we going to complete our challenge now?" Robbie sighed.

The tour ended at the souvenir shop.
Janie spotted some stuffed toys. Among
them were toy koalas. "I'm going to get
one of those!" she said.

"Those are for little kids," Robbie
protested. "I'm going to use my money to
buy candy."

"Think about it," Janie said. "Mom didn't
say we had to get our photo taken with a
real koala, did she?"

Janie bought a toy koala and they asked
a ranger to take their picture.

"You knew we wouldn't be able to get

our photo taken with a real koala, didn't you, Mom?" Laura asked.

Mom nodded. "That was the challenge!"

"We've learned a lot about real koalas!" said Robbie.

Janie hugged the koala toy. "And I've got a cuddly koala to keep as a souvenir!" she added.

The Knight

After a good night's sleep, Mistress Swift
helped Joe and Chee prepare for their
long journey to Duchess Enara's castle,
far away in the Eastern Hills of Neeve.

"Take care of each other. There are enemy soldiers everywhere," said Mistress Swift, putting a blanket and some food into a backpack for Joe.

"Don't worry," said Chee. "I'm tough. I'll look after both of us!"

Joe smiled as he hoisted Chee up to sit in the backpack and waved goodbye to Mistress Swift.

All day Joe and Chee walked up and down, hill after hill. At last, the furthest hill was ahead of them. On top of it was a castle.

"There it is!" said Chee. "The Castle of East Neeve."

A wide river flowed along the valley beneath. They made their way down to the bridge but, as they reached it, Joe stopped. "Listen!" he said. Slow, heavy footsteps were coming toward them. Chee ducked down into the backpack. "Who's there?" Joe called, his heart thumping with fear. He curled his fingers around the dragon-claw horn. Would he need to use it now?

A tall knight in shiny silver armor came out from behind a large weeping willow. "I am the Keeper of the Bridge," he boomed. "The duchess of East Neeve

113

commands that you pay fifty gold coins
to cross the river."

Joe looked up at the knight in dismay.

"We don't have any money," he said.

"Then you'll have to fight me to cross the
bridge," said the knight.

"He's awfully tall, isn't he?" Chee
whispered from the backpack.

"I know," Joe whispered back. "I'd never
beat him in a fight."

Chee climbed out of the backpack and
jumped to the ground.

"Well," said the knight. "Are you going to fight me?"

"No!" Joe replied. "Fighting's stupid."

"Unfortunately I don't agree," said the knight. Swish! The sword plunged into the ground near Chee.

"No!" Joe cried. He looked around and grabbed the biggest stick he could see. Swish! The knight's sword came down again. Joe thrust out his stick and stopped the blade from hitting Chee.

The knight turned and swung his sword at Joe.

Joe ducked and then ducked again. "Run away, Chee!" he yelled. "You don't have to prove how tough you are!"

115

"No way!" shouted Chee. "Watch this!" He ran at the knight, leaped up, and grabbed his belt. To Joe's amazement, Chee started to tickle him.

"Hee hoo har! Stop that!" the knight roared, laughing helplessly. But Chee didn't stop. The knight laughed so hard he fell over—and fell in half!

Two goblins wriggled out from the shiny suit of armor.

Joe grabbed one of them by the arm.
"Are you working for King Barzan?" he demanded.

"Me?" squeaked the goblin. "Oh no! We just wanted some gold. Stealing is easier than working."

"We'll see what the duchess thinks about this," said Joe firmly.

Duchess Enara was very angry with the goblins and sent them to clean her stinky cages as a punishment. "This explains why we've had so few visitors recently," she exclaimed. "But Chee, how did you know that the knight wasn't really a knight?"

"I didn't," said Chee. "But I couldn't let Joe face the knight all on his own, and it was the best plan I could think of."

"Well, I think you're both very brave," said the duchess warmly. "How can I reward you?"

Joe explained about the picture.

The duchess smiled. "I've kept that piece of paper safe in my castle for ten years," she said, "I'll be glad to give it to you." Joe's heart beat fast as he took the piece of parchment from the duchess. He looked closely at it—he could just about make out part of a drawing that looked like his home town.

He smiled at Chee. "Only two more pieces to go!" he said. "Are you ready to go again?"

Swimming: Perfect Race

"How's your swimming practice going?" Sophie asked her brother, as she scooped up a spoonful of cereal.

Daniel shrugged. "I'm not getting any faster and the school swim meet is only three weeks away."

He picked up his book bag.

"Adam Blade's pretty good," Sophie observed. "You'll have to work hard to beat him."

"I know," Daniel replied as he left for the pool. "He practices every morning, like me."

Daniel had set his heart on winning the 200-meter freestyle race. He wanted the prize: four free tickets to see any movie he wanted. But so did Adam Blade. Daniel shivered as he stood with his toes over the edge of the pool. Adam was already speeding through the water.

He swam through the water slowly at first. As his muscles grew warm he began to swim faster. He passed Adam a few times, but then just as many times, Adam passed him.

"Daniel!" a muffled voice shouted. Daniel finished his lap and looked up. It was Sophie. "What are you doing here?" he asked.

Sophie dangled her feet in the water. "I came to watch you practice," she replied. Daniel sighed. "I think I'm losing time in my turns," he said.

Sophie looked over at Adam. She
watched as he came to the end of a
lap, flipped over, and pushed away from
the wall. "Wow," she said. "Did you
see that?"

Daniel watched Adam swim to the other
side of the pool. "See what?" he asked.

"Adam's turns are perfect," Sophie told
him. "He hardly slows down. Watch."

Adam performed another rapid turn and headed toward them.

Daniel was quiet as he studied Adam's swimming stroke. "You know, if he kept his legs straighter and pointed his toes more, he would swim faster."

Sophie nodded. "And if you improved your turns, you'd make better time too."

Adam reached the end of the pool.

Daniel cupped his hands around his mouth. "Adam!" he yelled.

Adam stopped. He shook water from his hair and looked at the twins.

"I have an idea," Daniel told him. "I can help you improve your stroke if you help me with my turns."

Adam looked uncertain at first.

And then he pulled himself out of the pool and sat on the side. "Sounds good to me," he grinned.

Swimming Meet

A few days later it was the day of the swimming meet.

"The 200-meter freestyle," Coach Travers announced. "Swimmers, take your positions."

Daniel took his place at the end of the pool. Adam did the same.

The whistle blew and Daniel hit the water. He sped to the other end of the pool, remembering what Adam had taught him: he had to get closer to the wall before he turned, so he could get a stronger push with his legs.

Getting as close to the wall as he could, Daniel flipped over and pushed off again. Adam was right beside him in the next lane. Adam's stroke had speeded up too, thanks to Daniel's advice. Daniel pushed himself harder. But he couldn't shake off Adam. There he was—side by side with Daniel, length after length.

At last, Daniel's hand slapped against the tiles. The race was over. He stood up. Beside him, Adam did the same.

Who had won?

Coach Travers looked at her stopwatch and walked toward the boys, a huge smile on her face. "You have both broken your own records!" she told them. "And you both hold the new one!"

"Both of us?" asked Adam.

"It was a tie?" asked Daniel.

"That's right," said Coach Travers. "Congratulations! You share the prize between you. Two movie tickets each. Nice work, boys!"

The Mountain Mission

Jed was helping Ann the babysitter
prepare dinner when Mom arrived home.
She came into the kitchen, and put two
plane tickets onto the table.
"Surprise! We're flying to Switzerland
first thing tomorrow," she said. "So we'd
better start packing!"
"Are we going skiing?" asked Jed
excitedly.

"Yes, we're staying in a luxury ski resort," replied Mom.

"Wow!" said Ann.

Jed was curious. Why had his mom suddenly decided to take this vacation? It must have something to do with her work, he guessed.

While Mom was packing, Jed sneaked upstairs, turned on her computer, and checked her emails.

He soon found out why they were really going. Some plans for a new spy plane had been stolen and Mom's mission was to get them back. An enemy agent called Max Blatt had the plans in his Swiss mountain hideout.

"This could be Mom's most dangerous mission yet," Jed said to himself. "Good job I'm going along too."

"Wow!" said Jed, as they arrived in the ski resort. He almost forgot why they were really there as he looked up at the

snow-covered mountains. He couldn't
wait to put his skis on and get out on
those ski runs. He loved skiing.

Mom was looking up, too. Jed followed
her gaze. She was staring at a building at
the top of a nearby mountain.

"That must be Blatt's hideout," Jed
guessed. It was a long way up. Jed knew
that his mom wasn't very good at skiing.

She'd never make it down that mountain. "I have to act fast, before Mom tries anything stupid," he said to himself. While Mom was unpacking, Jed went to explore the resort. Spotting a store that sold costumes, he had an idea. He took out the money he'd brought with him, paid for a St Bernard dog costume, and then smuggled it into his room.

"At least this silly disguise will keep me warm in the snow!" Jed thought as he put

on the furry outfit the following morning.

There was only one way up the mountain, in the ski lift. Some skiers laughed when Jed got in, dressed in his costume.

"I didn't know dogs could ski!" one of
them joked.
At the top of the mountain, Jed left the
skiers behind. He made his way to the
security fence surrounding Blatt's hideout
and climbed over it.

131

Sneaking in through an open window, Jed found Blatt's office, and began to look around for the plans.
"They must be in here somewhere," he thought.

Suddenly three large dogs appeared. Jed was about to run when he saw that they didn't look at all fierce. They wanted to make friends.

"My costume must have fooled them," Jed thought with a relieved grin.

He found the plans, grabbed them, and ran to the back door, almost tripping over a dog bed. "That will come in handy!" he said, picking it up.

It was great fun sledding down the

mountain in the dog bed.

Soon Jed was back in his hotel. He went up to the reception desk.

"Will you send these papers up to Frances Best in Room 303, please?" he asked, handing over the plans.

"Mom will love the room service in this hotel!" Jed laughed to himself.

The Cinderella Problem

Kayla's little sister, Molly, had broken her leg.

"Molly needs to be cheered up," Kayla told the others when they gathered in the garage. "She was supposed to see *Cinderella* at the movies this afternoon.

But now she can't go with her friend and his family."

"Poor Molly!" said Ava. "She must be really disappointed."

Emily chewed her thumb. "Well, we all know the story of Cinderella, don't we?" she said.

"Maybe *we* could put on a surprise show for Molly this afternoon."

They hurried into the house to tell Kayla's mom. Molly was in the living room, watching TV with Jordan and Tom. She looked at her leg in a cast and sniffed sadly.

Kayla's mom thought the surprise show was a great idea. "I'll make some phone calls and invite people over," she said.

"We need Cinderella, Prince Charming, and a fairy godmother," said Emily. She turned to Ava. "You're the tallest, Ava. You should be Prince Charming."

Ava nodded. "I'll wear my crown."

"I'll be the fairy godmother," said Mia. "My sister's got some fairy wings and a wand."

"Great," said Emily. "Kayla, you be Cinderella. I'll be the clock to chime out midnight. I'll make a clock mask."

"I'll wear my old party dress,"

agreed Kayla. "And you can use Jordan's trumpet for the chimes."

The girls hurried off to get everything they needed. Back at the garage, Kayla showed the others a huge, hollowed-out pumpkin.

"Cinderella's coach!" she said. "Dad did it for us. We'll fix it onto a skateboard and Bouncer can pull it along!"

"Are you sure Bouncer will know what to do?" Mia asked doubtfully.

"He'll be fine!" Kayla smiled.

She gave Emily Jordan's toy trumpet. "And look," she said. "I borrowed Tom's toy cat for poor, cold Cinderella at the beginning."

The next hour flashed by. People began to arrive. Kayla's dad popped his head into the garage. "Your audience awaits, girls,"

he said
with a smile.
"We'd better
start," said
Kayla. "If we
get stuck, just
make something
up!" She flung
a shawl over
her party dress,
picked up Tom's
toy cat and
walked right

out onto the lawn.

"I'm so sad," she said. "My sisters have gone to the ball and I have only my cat to keep me warm."

Tom was sitting on the grass in front of the chairs. "*Kayla!* That's *my* cat!" he shouted loudly.

"Be quiet! I promise I'll give it back to you after the show," Kayla hissed.

Mia hurried out of the house, waving her wand. "I'm your fairy godmother," she said. "Take that shawl off. Your old dress is now a beautiful gown, Cinderella. You *shall* go to the ball. But you must be back by midnight."

Music began to play. Ava stepped out. "I'm Prince Charming," she said to Kayla as they began to dance together. Emily came out in the clock mask, blowing the trumpet.

"That's *my* trumpet!" yelled Jordan.

Kayla rolled her eyes. "I'll give it

back after the show," she hissed. "It's
midnight!" she cried, and ran to the other
side of the lawn. "Oh no! My coach has
turned back into a pumpkin!"
"Here, Bouncer!" Mia shouted.
Bouncer came shooting out from behind
the shed, barking loudly and pulling the
pumpkin behind him.
The audience roared with laughter.
Ava knelt before Kayla and held her
hand. "I don't care that you're poor,

Cinderella. I want you to be my
princess."

"And everyone lived happy ever after,"
shouted Jordan. "*Now* can I have my
trumpet back?"

The audience cheered and clapped—and
Molly made the loudest noise of all!

Kingston Clue

Laura, Robbie, and Janie were very sad to be leaving Australia—until Dad told them they were going to Kingston, Jamaica!

"You're going to have so much fun here," Dad said, as the plane touched down on the Caribbean island.

The next day Dad went off to rehearse and everyone else went to the beach. While Mom read a book and sunbathed, Laura, Janie, and Robbie joined in the beach volleyball and then cooled down in the clear blue ocean.

"I wonder what our challenge is going to be," Janie said, floating on her back.

"I don't know, but I hope we can do it here on the beach," Laura answered.

For lunch they had jerk chicken followed by delicious fresh fruit that had just been picked. There were bananas, pineapples, and mangoes, and some fruits they didn't even know the names of.

"I think you'll like your next challenge," Mom said, when they had finished eating. "I want you to find me an object that will remind me of Jamaica when I get home."

"What a nice challenge," Janie said, when Mom had gone back to her book. "I've already thought of the answer!" said Laura. "Let's give Mom a freshly

picked pineapple to remind her of
Jamaica."

"We have canned pineapple all the time
at home," Robbie replied. "Let's get her
a mango instead."

Janie looked doubtful. "But she won't
be able to keep a pineapple *or* a mango
for ever," she said. "They'll go all soft
and rotten."

"You're right," Laura agreed.

"We'll have to think of something else,"
said Robbie.

"We're going to explore the market
today," Mom said, the next morning.

146

The market was very busy. Some stalls were piled high with fruit and vegetables, and fish caught just that morning. Others sold brightly colored scarves and skirts, little wooden statues and boxes, or jewelry made of beads.

"Let's get Mom a scarf," Janie suggested. "It will remind her of Jamaica for ever, because she'll know we bought it from here."

"Quick then," Janie said. "Let's choose one while she's not looking."

"Let's get that one," Robbie said, pointing to a red and green one.

"No!" Laura objected. "The blue and yellow one. It will look better on her."

"I think the purple one's the prettiest," said Janie.

"There you are!" said Mom's voice from behind them.

They turned around. Mom held up a beautiful green and gold scarf.

"Look what I just bought myself!" she said, smiling. "Isn't it pretty?"

"Now we'll have to think of something else!" Robbie said.

That afternoon they went back to the beach again.

"This is my favorite place in Jamaica," said Mom, sighing happily.

"That's it!" Laura whispered. "We have to find something that will remind Mom of the beach here in Jamaica."

Laura spotted a conch shell near the ocean's edge.
She ran over and picked it up. It was a beautiful creamy white, tinged with pink. "Let's give her this!" she said.
"Look, Mom…" Laura

explained. "It's beautiful. Best of all, if you hold it to your ear you can hear the sound of the ocean!"

Mom held the shell to her ear. "So I can," she said with a smile. "But we can't take this, because you shouldn't take shells from beaches."

"Oh," said Robbie, unhappily.

"I guess we've failed this challenge."

Mom smiled and pulled her camera out of her bag. "But I can take a picture of it!" she said. "That will do just as well to remind me of Jamaica."

Goblin Trouble

On their way to Duke Oskar's castle in the Western Hills, Joe and Chee stopped under a huge old tree to rest and eat the food given to them by Duchess Enara. Suddenly, a boy and girl came running out of the nearby woods.

"Help!" cried the girl, when she saw Joe and Chee. "Is there somewhere to hide? Goblins are chasing us!"

"The tree!" Chee shouted, pointing to the tree's hollowed-out trunk.

They all hurried inside the tree trunk. Peering out, Joe saw a group of young goblins mounted on fierce-looking wolves racing out of the woods. He held his breath as they got nearer and nearer. Soon the wolves were sniffing around on the grass near the tree trunk itself.

"They must be somewhere around here," growled the lead goblin. "Or the wolves wouldn't have stopped. Don't worry, Dolph and Maya, we'll find you!" he shouted. Joe gulped.

But at that moment the goblins' voices were drowned out by a massive roar—from further *inside* the tree! The noise was as loud as thunder.

"It's a troll!" Maya exclaimed. They shrank back as the massive, stinky creature lumbered past. Fortunately, the troll was only interested in the goblins.

"Who dares disturb me?" the troll roared, grabbing at them. Shrieking and yelping, the goblins and their wolves fled.

Then one of the goblins slipped and fell. The troll scooped the goblin up, and raised him to his huge mouth.

"He's going to eat him!" gasped Dolph. "I know he's a goblin, but we have to do something!"

Chee made an ear-piercing whistle. With another great roar, the troll dropped the goblin and stomped off, holding his ears.

"Works every time with trolls," Chee said.

Joe hurried over to the goblin. His leg was badly hurt.

"We can't leave him here," said Dolph.

"If you can just take me to the edge of Goblin Grove, no one will see you," said the young goblin.

As they got near to gloomy Goblin Grove, Joe's heart began to beat fast.

"Leave me here," whispered the goblin, when they reached a crooked tree.

Too late! A voice barked, "Who goes there?" and a large goblin holding a sharp spear stepped out from behind the tree.

"Duke Oskar's children!" he said, as he saw Maya and Dolph. "I think you'll be coming with me."

"Send the duke a message saying he can have his children back if he gives his land to King Barzan," the goblin chief commanded, when the captives were brought before him. "And throw them in prison!"

But a little while later a key turned in the lock. The goblin boy they had helped crept in. "Quick!" he whispered. "I've unlocked the back gate and the guard's asleep—go! You saved my life, and I can't leave you here."

As they were tiptoeing out of the back gate, a wolf howled and woke the guard up.

"Run!" shouted Joe. They ran as fast as they could, but soon the goblins on their wolves were catching up.

Joe pulled out the dragon-claw horn. He blew on it hard. No sound came out! Had it worked? The wolves were so close now that Joe could see their glowing eyes.

He stared up into the sky. A tiny speck appeared high above. It grew bigger and bigger. The dragon!

It swooped down with a terrible roar and the goblins scattered, screaming in fear. Then Joe heard the thunder of horses' hooves. "Look!" he called. In the distance was a group of horsemen.

"It's Father and his men coming to rescue us!" cried Maya.

"This is Joe," Dolph explained to his father. "He saved us from the goblins!"

"My sister sent a messenger to say you were coming," said the duke. "It looks as though you're every bit as brave as she said you were. And before you ask— yes, I do have the second piece of the picture!"

Track and Field: Surprise Star

"Oh, no! We've got Jasmine," Jason whispered to Daniel and Sophie. "She's hopeless." The class was about to play basketball.

"Give her a chance," Sophie said. Staring at her shoes, Jasmine walked over to her team.

Coach Travers held up the basketball. "Ready?" she called. Then she blew her whistle.

During the game, Sophie saw Jasmine back away whenever the ball came near. But then, near the end of the game, Daniel yelled, "Jasmine! You're closest to the net!" He threw the ball to her.

"Catch it!" yelled Jason.

Jasmine ran forward, holding out her arms as far as she could.

Sophie held her breath.

The ball slipped through Jasmine's hands and bounced off the ground.

Sammy on the other team grabbed it and headed off down to the other end of the court at a fast pace. He steered the ball up into the air and it dropped nice and neatly into the net.

"Score!" his team shouted.

Coach Travers blew her whistle loudly. The game was over.

After the game Sophie watched Jasmine trudge gloomily away from the gym. She hurried to catch up with her. "Cheer up, Jasmine," she said. "It's supposed to be fun."

"I know," Jasmine replied quietly. "But I'm terrible at basketball." She shrugged and walked away with her head down.

"Did you hear about the charity fun run?" Daniel asked Sophie as they walked home. "You collect sponsors and run laps around the school track."
Just then, Jasmine sprinted around the corner with her older brother. Both of them had bags full of newspapers bouncing against their backs.

Sophie stopped, her eyes wide. "Look!" she said. "See how fast Jasmine is!"
"Maybe *she* should enter the fun run," said Daniel.
Sophie nodded and began running after Jasmine. "Hey! Jasmine!" she called.
Jasmine stopped, allowing Sophie and Daniel to catch up.

"You're so fast!" Sophie panted.
Jasmine shrugged. "We run to get the paper round finished quickly," she said.
"Well, we think you should enter the fun run," Daniel told her.
Now Jasmine looked surprised. "But I'm terrible at sports," she protested.
"You're not terrible at running, and that's a sport," Sophie pointed out.
Daniel patted Jasmine's paper bag. "Think about it," he said. "You're training every day, helping your brother with this job."
Jasmine shuffled her feet and looked down. "I'll think about it," she said.

On the morning of the fun run, Sophie and Daniel lined up with the other runners. Daniel nudged Sophie.

"Jasmine's here," he said, pointing to the other side of the crowd.

Sophie smiled. "Great!" she said.

"I really hoped she would be."

"Ready, runners?" Coach Travers called. "You have one hour."

The starting whistle blew!

Sophie and Daniel began to run. A few seconds later, Jasmine ran past.

After thirty minutes, at least half of the runners had dropped out and were sitting at the sidelines watching the rest of the fun run. After fifty minutes, only a few were left running. And still way out in front was Jasmine sprinting ahead.

Coach Travers blew her whistle. "That's one hour!" she announced.

Jasmine came and sank onto the grass next to Sophie and Daniel. "You were right!" she beamed. "Running is a sport I *can* do well."

"Runners, gather around, please!" called Coach Travers.

"You have all run like champions," she said, "but the highest number of laps was run by… Jasmine!"

Everyone cheered and clapped. Coach Travers looked very happy.

"And now that Jasmine has shown us what she can do, I hope she will join our cross-country team," Coach Travers added.

Jasmine smiled with happiness. "Yes, please!" she said.

The Gadget Meeting

"Can I have a new cell phone for my birthday?" Jed asked Mom. "One that takes pictures and plays music? Some even have a TV screen!" he added hopefully. Jed loved gadgets.

Mom looked up from her computer. "Have you seen how much they cost?" she said. "I'm sorry, Jed, they're just too expensive."

Jed sighed loudly. It was OK for Mom, he thought. She could use cool gadgets whenever she liked. It was part of her job as a secret agent.

"Time for dinner," said Mom. She stood up and went downstairs.

Jed sat down at the computer, wondering if the screen would show him Mom's latest mission.

It didn't. The email on screen was from Aunt Kathy, asking Mom what to get Jed for his birthday. Jed thought about replying as Mom and suggesting a new cell phone. He grinned. Better not.

Just then, Jed noticed an email marked TOP SECRET higher up in Mom's inbox. He clicked on it.

Dear Agent
The latest spy tools and gadgets will be shown tomorrow.
Time: 2:00 p.m., Saturday July 16th.
Place: The Windsor Room, Royal Hotel, Buckingham Palace Road, London.
All agents must attend.

"Wow…" Jed sighed. "Lucky Mom!" he thought.

"Hurry up, Jed!" shouted Mom.
Jed jumped—and accidentally clicked on "Delete."
"Oh no!" he gasped. He hoped that Mom would remember the address in the email. Jed couldn't tell her, or she would guess what he had been up to!

That night, Mom spent hours on the computer. And the next morning she looked very worried.

"Are you going to work today, Mom?" Jed asked.

Mom shook her head.

Jed said nothing, but he felt very guilty. Then he had an idea. If he couldn't tell her where the secret meeting was, maybe he could show her.

"Can we go on a bus tour around London?" he asked. "It's a sunny day."

"OK," said Mom. "It might cheer me up."

The bus tour went on a loop, passing
all the famous landmarks. As the bus
got close to Buckingham Palace, Jed
wondered if his plan would work. He
looked at his watch. It was 1:50.
Just then, Mom gasped. She was staring
at the Royal Hotel. She had remembered!
"Jed, I've just seen some friends from
work I want to say hello to," she said,

standing up. "Stay on the bus and see the rest of the tour. I'll meet you back here." "OK, Mom," said Jed, smiling as she hurried off the bus. "See you later." But Jed got off the bus at the next stop. He walked back up Buckingham Palace Road and into the Royal Hotel. "I'll just have to make sure Mom doesn't see me in here!" he said.

Jed had the best time trying out some amazing gadgets. "This is even better than that cell phone I wanted," he said, picking up a satellite tracking device. He typed in Mom's name—and a picture of her came up on the screen.

She was standing at the bus stop outside!
"Oops, I'd better go!" he said. He put
the gadget down and hurried out. "Hi,
Mom!" he said, tapping her gently on
the back.
"Where have you been?" she cried. "The
bus came, but you weren't on it!"

"Sorry, Mom," Jed replied. "I suddenly got car sick so I got off a couple of stops early. I had to walk all the way up Buckingham Palace Road!"

Jed's mom gave him a hug. "Poor thing!" she said. "Let's go to the movies. There's a new spy movie playing."

"Great!" Jed agreed. This had turned out to be a perfect day.

Clothes Swap

Isabella was handing out invitations in class.

Ava read her invitation. "Wow, a birthday square dancing party!" she said.

"Thanks, Isabella!" said Mia.

Isabella smiled. "I'm inviting the whole class," she said. "Don't wear anything fancy. Tee shirts, jeans, and boots would be great."

Everyone smiled and nodded.

Then Emily started to chew her thumb.

"Uh-oh, Emily's thinking," said Mia.

"What's going on inside your head, Em?" asked Kayla.

"Well, I know Isabella said not to wear  anything dressy to her party... but I'd like something new to wear," Emily admitted.

"Me, too," said Kayla. "I mean, I've got some

cool tee shirts, but everybody has seen them lots of times."

Mia and Ava nodded in agreement.

"We'll have to use our allowance to buy Isabella birthday presents," said Ava. "So if we are going to buy some cool new tee shirts too, we are going to need to earn some more money."

The girls helped mow the grass in Emily's dad's yard (VERY HARD WORK!). They painted a fence for Ava's grandma (GOOD FUN!). They dusted Ava's mom's knick knacks (TRICKY). Finally, they did a HUGE amount of dishes for Emily's mom.

At last, the girls had earned enough money to buy a tee shirt each.

Ava's big sister, Madison, offered to take the girls on their shopping trip. They decided to go to a coffee shop before they started shopping. The friends were so excited that, somehow, a glass of triple chocolate milkshake got knocked over on the table. The brown, sticky liquid went all over Madison's suede skirt.

"Oh, no!" she cried. "My new skirt's ruined! The stain will never come out."

Ava bit her lip and looked at the others.

The Cupcake Club all guessed what she was thinking. The four girls got out the money

they'd earned and gave it to Madison to help pay for a new skirt.

Back at the garage, they wrapped the presents they had each bought for Isabella and wrote on her cards.

"We'll just have to wear our old stuff," Mia said with a sigh.

Suddenly, Ava stopped wrapping. "I've got a great idea!" she said. "We'll have to check with our moms first. But if they agree, why don't we have a clothes swap?"

"Cool!" grinned Kayla. "A fashion makeover."

The friends arrived back at the garage and piled the tee shirts and jeans they wanted to swap on the table.

Ava went first because it had been her idea. She chose a striped tee shirt Emily had brought. "So I go next," said Emily. "I'll take these black jeans."

"I brought them," said Kayla. "My turn

now." Kayla chose a blue tee shirt.
"Excellent!" Mia yelled. "That means I
can have this yellow tee shirt."
The next day, Ava had a surprise for
the others. "Madison gave me the skirt
we ruined," she told them. "I used the
unstained pieces to make suede belts—
and fringes to stick on our boots!"
"Ava! That was another great idea," said
Emily.

"Sure was," Mia and Kayla agreed as they started sticking the fringes in place. Mia's dad was driving the girls to Isabella's. "Great boots, girls," he said as the friends scrambled into the car. "They're just the thing for a square dance!"

New York Night

The band's next concert was in New
York City. After the beach everyone
was excited to be in such a busy city. At
breakfast on the first morning they talked
about what they wanted to do.

"I'd like to go on a boat ride around the Statue of Liberty," said Janie.

"I'd like to go to the top of the Empire State Building," Robbie put in.

"And I'd like to go to the zoo in Central

Park," Laura said.

"OK, we can do all that," Mom said. "But first, I have to give you your final challenge." She looked around at them and smiled. "My favorite singer, Amber, is here in New York! She has a concert tonight, and I want you to get her autograph."

"Dad could help us get it easily," Robbie said right away.

"But that would be cheating!" Dad said, pretending to be shocked.

"This challenge is going to be hard," said Janie as she, Laura, and Robbie waited for Mom in the hotel lobby. Dad had gone off to rehearsals, as usual.

"We could buy tickets for Amber's concert and then go backstage afterward," Robbie suggested.

"Us and about ten million other people," Laura replied. "It's not like we can use Dad's name or anything."

"Someone must know where we might find her," said Janie. "She can't just stay inside all day."

The hotel doorman seemed to know everyone. Robbie asked him about Amber.

"Sure," he said. "When Amber's in New York, she walks her little dog in Central Park around eleven o'clock."

Robbie looked at his watch—ten-thirty! He told Laura and Janie, and they hurried upstairs to ask Mom to take them to Central Park.

Central Park was huge but luckily the doorman had told them exactly where to find Amber.

"There she is!" said Laura, pointing to a woman in a pink sweatsuit and sunglasses. She was walking a tiny dog on a jeweled leash, and was surrounded by three huge bodyguards.

Robbie, Janie, and Laura went up to one of the bodyguards.

"Please can we have Amber's autograph?" Laura asked.

"Sorry, kid," the bodyguard said.
"Amber doesn't want to be bothered today."
"There must be something we can do," Janie said to the others.
"I hope so!" said Mom.
Then Robbie spotted an old lady sitting on a bench. She had a tiny poodle on a leash.
"That's a nice dog," he said to her.

"Could we take him for a walk?"
The old lady smiled. "Fifi would love that," she said.
While Robbie, Janie, and Laura hurried after Amber and her bodyguards, Mom stayed to talk with the old lady.
Fifi and Amber's little dog were very excited when they saw each other.

"What a cute little poodle!" Amber exclaimed.

Soon, Robbie, Janie, and Laura were talking to Amber as if they were all old friends.

"I have to go now," Amber said after a while. "Nice to meet you."

Robbie realized they had nearly forgotten something!

"Could we have your autograph please, Amber?" he asked.

"Sure," Amber replied.

That afternoon, a pleased Mom showed the autograph to Dad.

"Good job!" he said to Robbie, Janie, and Laura. "And guess what! You'll be meeting your new friend again this evening. We're all going to Amber's concert!"

After the concert, Dad took them all backstage.

"I know you!" Amber exclaimed when she saw Robbie, Laura, and Janie. "You're the ones who had that cute poodle in the park today."

Mountain Adventure

Joe and Chee set off on their final journey to Duke Gregor's castle, up in the snow-capped mountains of Northern Neeve. New snowfall began to hide the mountain path they were on.

"I think we might be lost," said Chee in a small voice.

Joe could see a faint light in the distance.
"I think that might be a cabin," he said.
"Let's ask for help."
When Joe knocked on the cabin door
a man opened it. "Come in!" he said,
seeing Joe and Chee shivering on his
doorstep. "You must be freezing!"
A boy and girl were warming bread in the
flames of a fire.

"I'm Kala," said the girl. "And this is Dalin." The boy smiled.

"And I'm Tor," said the man.

"We can show you the way to Duke Gregor's castle in the morning, but we can't take you there," said Kala.

"We have all been banished," added Dalin bitterly.

Their father sighed. "I used to look after Duke Gregor's diamond mine. But some diamonds disappeared and Duke Gregor thinks I stole them," he explained.

"So he made us leave the village," Kala went on. "And now we have to live here, on the other side of the mountain."

After a dinner of toast, cheese, and mountain berries, Joe and Chee spent a cozy night in front of the fire.

The following morning they set off with Kala and Dalin. As they reached the top of the mountain they could see the Castle of Northern Neeve in the valley below, surrounded by a busy village.

Suddenly, Kala gasped. "There he is," she whispered to Dalin. She pointed at a man with a long red beard who was climbing up the mountain.

"Who is he?" Chee asked.

"That's Jamar," said Dalin. "He now has Father's job at the diamond mine. Father thinks he stole the diamonds, but no one will listen to us."

Joe shook his head. "That's terrible!" he said angrily.

He thought for a second. "Chee and I could follow Jamar and look for proof that he's the thief," he offered.

"Yes, Jamar won't suspect us," Chee added eagerly.

Joe and Chee followed Jamar to a cave hidden high in the mountainside. They waited and watched until he came out again and headed back toward the village.

"Now's our chance," said Joe.

He and Chee slipped into the cave.

Through the shadows, Joe could see a large wooden chest.

He lifted the lid and gasped. Inside was a heap of glittering diamonds. There was a letter inside too.

It was from King Barzan, telling Jamar where to send the diamonds—so that they could be used to pay his army. Chee whistled softly. "So Jamar works for King Barzan…" he said.

"I'm sure Duke Gregor will find this very interesting!" said Joe. "Let's take this down to the castle."

"Look at these!" said Joe, handing the letter and a handful of the diamonds to the duke.

Duke Gregor stared at the diamonds and the letter. "Find Jamar and throw him in the dungeon!" he ordered his guards. "And then bring Tor and his family to me. I've done them a great wrong. They can return to live in the village."

He turned to Joe and Chee. "The Land of Neeve is most grateful to you," he said. "Now our enemy King Barzan won't be able to pay his army, the war will soon be over. What can I do to reward you?"

Joe asked Duke Gregor for the final piece of the picture.

"Of course!" said Duke Gregor.

Joe's heart thumped with excitement.

Finally, he was going home.
When the piece of picture was found, Joe quickly fitted all three pieces together.
He felt himself starting to fall...

Snowboarding:
Try it, You'll Like it!

It was the last day of school before the winter vacation. Sophie and Daniel were really excited.

"We're taking snowboarding lessons over the vacation," Sophie told their classmates.

"Me too," said Jason.

"What have you planned, Amir?" Daniel asked.

"Let me guess," Jason interrupted. "Playing computer games—right, Amir?" Amir looked up from his work and grinned. "Good guess," he answered. "I'm not into winter sports stuff. While you three are out there on the slopes, I'll be nice and cozy—playing *Snowboard Safari* on my laptop!"

Ten days later, it was time for the first snowboarding lesson. Daniel and Sophie pulled on their goggles, hats, and gloves, and then grabbed their boards and clumped outside. A small group was gathered nearby, and a man with a clipboard called out names.

"Daniel and Sophie Lutz?"

"Here!" Daniel and Sophie said.

"Jason Walker?"

"Here!" Jason called back.

"Amir Mahmood?"

Daniel and Sophie looked at each other in surprise.

"Amir Mahmood?" the instructor called out again.

"I'm here," he said. "I thought you weren't into winter sports," Daniel whispered.

"I'm not," Amir whispered back, grumpily. "My parents didn't want me to spend the vacation in front of the computer so they gave me boarding lessons as a surprise."

The class spent the next thirty minutes in one spot. They learned how to stand, balance and lean on the snowboard.

"Ready to try the real thing?" the instructor asked.

"Yes!" shouted most of the group.

"Not really," muttered Amir.

They followed the instructor to the rope tow that would carry them to the top of the beginners' slope.

"Sophie, you first," the instructor said. "Just grab the cable, lean back a little, and let it pull you up the hill."

At the top, Daniel and Sophie stood with Amir and Jason.

"Ready?" Daniel said.

"It looks steep," Amir replied.

Sophie pointed her board sideways and bent her knees. Daniel and Jason did the same. Amir just watched.

"Let's go!" Sophie said.

She slid a few feet and then fell backward into the snow.

Jason raced past her. "I'm going too fast!" he yelled. He swerved and tumbled into a snow bank.

"Not any more!" Sophie called.

Daniel laughed and then turned to Amir. "Your turn next!" he said.

But Amir shook his head. "In a minute," he replied.

Daniel pushed off to catch up with Sophie. Together, they slipped, stumbled, and rolled down the hill.

"Let's go again!" Sophie said at the bottom. When they got to the top, Amir was still waiting.

"Come on, Amir," Sophie said. "We're all clumsy!"

Amir smiled. He took a step forward. "I guess if you can fall down the hill, I can too." He pointed his board, bent his knees, and started to slide forwards.

"That's it, Amir!" Daniel called.
"Hey, Amir!" Sophie called. "You've
gone further than I did!"
But just then, Amir slipped off his board
into the snow.
"He's down," said Daniel. "Let's go."
Daniel and Sophie headed down to help
Amir up, but they were too slow.
By the time they reached the spot where

he had fallen, he was on his board again and halfway down the hill.

Sophie slid the last few feet on her knees. Daniel skidded into her and they fell in a laughing heap.

Amir walked over to them. "This is much better than *Snowboard Safari*," he said. "What are you waiting for? Come on! Let's go again!"

The Double Agent

Jed was playing in an important soccer game at school.

"I'll come and watch!" Mom said that morning, as she left for work. But when Jed scanned the crowd of cheering parents, his mom was nowhere to be seen. Ann was there instead.

"Where's Mom?" Jed asked, when the game was over. His team had lost 3-0, and Jed was in a bad mood.

"She called to say she had to stay late at work," Ann replied.

That night, Mom didn't get home until after Jed's bedtime. She came in and sat down on Jed's bed. "I'm really sorry about not coming to your soccer game, Jed," she said. "There are problems at work. I might lose my job if things don't get better." She looked tired and worried. Jed stopped feeling angry. Mom needs my help, he thought.

Later that night, Jed crept downstairs into the study. He clicked on Mom's inbox to see what had been happening.

The latest email was from Chief Officer Gridlock, Mom's boss.

Dear Agent

I am sorry to inform you that more government secrets have been leaked to the newspapers. You have failed in your mission to root out the double agent at Unit X. I am taking you off the case.

Gridlock

Jed sighed. Things really were bad.

The next morning, Jed didn't turn up for his paper route. Instead, he biked to Unit X. I'm going to have a good look around, he thought.

Jed slipped past the security guard
and up the stairs. He soon found Chief
Officer Gridlock's office, but Jed could
tell that Chief Officer Gridlock was
already inside. There was a light shining
under his door.
Jed waited around the corner. After a
few minutes, Gridlock's door opened. A
fierce-looking man came out and walked

across the hall to the bathroom. Jed
followed. Now's my chance, he thought,
as Gridlock shut the door. Jed wedged a
chair under the door knob.

"Who's that?" shouted Gridlock. "Let me
out at once!"
Jed ran back to Gridlock's office. There
wasn't a moment to lose. He needed a list
of all the people who worked at Unit X.
Gridlock had been checking his emails,
and had left them up on his screen. Jed
clicked on the "Sent" button.
He took a deep breath. "Gridlock doesn't

know much about computers!" he said. "He sends his emails to every one of his contacts—even the national newspaper editors. So he's the one accidentally giving away all the secrets!"

Suddenly a hand gripped Jed's shoulder. Gridlock wasn't the boss of Unit X for nothing: he had escaped from the bathroom. "Who on earth are you? I'm calling security!" Gridlock growled.

"Go on. I'll show them what you've done!" said Jed. "I know that you are the only double agent around here. These emails prove it!" Jed showed Gridlock what he'd found.

Gridlock sat down heavily in his chair. "I didn't mean to!" he groaned. "I've never understood computers."

"Then perhaps you should retire, and let someone take over who does," replied Jed. "And I know someone perfect for the job: Agent Frances Best."

Jed walked to the door. "If you don't tell on me, then I won't tell on you," he said. And then he hurried out.

That evening, Mom came home from work in a very happy mood. "I've gotten

a big promotion, Jed!" she told him.
Jed gave her a hug. "Good job, Mom!" he
said. Now he could look forward to some
even more exciting missions.
"I couldn't have done it without you,
Jed," Mom went on.
You don't know how true that is! Jed
thought with a grin.

The Present Problem

The best friends were sad when Ms Butler, their teacher, told them she'd be leaving soon.

Ava suggested they make her a going away present, and the others agreed it was a good idea.

"What do you think she would like?" Emily asked.

"Well, we know she loves snacks," said Kayla. "She told us so."

"I've got it!" cried Emily, jumping up.

"What did everyone love at Daniel's birthday party?" she asked.

"The rice krispie treats!" said Ava, Kayla and Mia together.

"And we can make a pretty box to put them in," said Emily.

The friends got together in Kayla's kitchen after school to make the rice krispie treats. They decorated a box to put the treats in, and made a large "Sorry You're Leaving" card.

"Perfect! Let's take them down to the clubhouse to keep them safe," said Kayla.

But next morning at school, Kayla had bad news. "I couldn't have closed the garage door right," she confessed. "Bouncer got in and ate all the rice krispie treats. He chewed the empty box, too."

"Oh no!" cried Mia. Ms Butler was leaving tomorrow, and they wouldn't have time to buy the ingredients to make more rice krispie treats after school that day. Kayla's grandma was arriving from Jamaica and they had all been invited to her "Welcome" party. They couldn't miss that.

After school, the friends all went around to Kayla's. Her grandma was showing her scrapbook full of amazing photographs taken when she was a girl in Jamaica.

She'd also stuck in other mementos:
newspaper clippings and tickets and
brochures from places she'd visited.
"I call it my memory book," Kayla's
grandma said with a smile.
Kayla looked over at Ava, Mia, and
Emily. "Are you thinking what I'm
thinking?" she asked.
"Yes!" the other three yelled.

They couldn't wait to start a memory book for Ms Butler.

"I've got a new note book in my room," said Kayla. "We can use that."

Ava was great at drawing. She drew cartoons of funny things that had happened while they were all in Ms Butler's class.

The friends also decided to put in some of the pictures they'd made in Ms Butler's art class and some of the poems they'd written in English class.

Emily waved a copy of the school magazine. "There's a big photo of us four at a School Spirit day in here," she said excitedly.

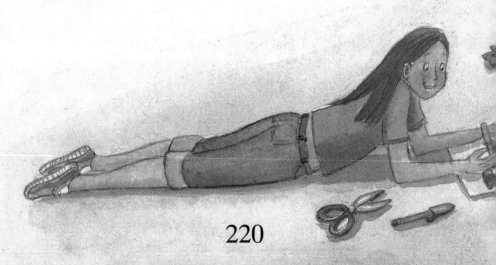

"Ms Butler is in it, too. And there are smaller photos of the rest of our class too!"

The next day, the friends gave Ms Butler the book and her going away card.

"It's a memory book," explained Ava. "So you'll always remember us!"

Ms Butler was delighted. "I'll treasure it always," she said.

Vancouver Victory

The band had nearly finished the tour. The last concert was in Vancouver, Canada.

Robbie, Laura, and Janie spent the morning biking with Mom in Stanley Park. It was very beautiful, with the ocean on one side and mountains on the other.

They fed the ducks and were amazed
when a raccoon with a black mask across
his furry face came to be fed too.
"We've completed all our challenges
now, Mom," said Robbie. "When are you
going to tell us about our special treat?"
"You'll have to wait just a little longer,"
Mom said with a smile. "Dad and I will
tell you tonight, after dinner."
None of them ate much at dinner because
they were so excited.

Finally, Mom put a bag on the dinner table. She opened it and took out the photograph of London that Janie took from the plane.

Next, she took out the chocolate mousse recipe that Robbie was given in the Paris café. "I'll make the mousse myself as soon as we get home," she said, with a smile.

Mom then took out the photograph of Robbie, Janie, and Laura hugging the toy koala they'd bought.

Next came the photograph of the conch shell. Mom held it up. "I can almost smell the ocean!" she said.

Lastly, Mom took out Amber's autograph. "That concert was great!" she said. "We've had so much fun with these challenges, haven't we?"

"Yes we have, but please will you tell us what our treat is?" Robbie said. "This is worse than waiting for Christmas!"

Mom and Dad laughed.

"All right," Mom said smiling. She put her hand into the bag one more time— and took out some airplane tickets. "We're not just flying straight home," Dad said. "We've bought around the world tickets for the way home! This time I don't have to work, so I can enjoy it with you."

"You all get to choose one place each to go," Mom added.

Laura, Robbie, and Janie were so excited that they all started to talk at once.

227

When they had calmed down, Mom said, "You first, Robbie."

"I want to go to Peru and see where the Incas lived," Robbie decided.

"I want to go to Switzerland," Laura said, "I've always wanted to see the mountains and the pretty chalet houses there."

"Iceland!" Janie exclaimed. "I want to see the geysers—and go on a boat to look at the whales."

"What about you?" Dad asked Mom. "This was all your idea, after all!"

"I want to go to Italy and find more pasta recipes!" Mom said. "How about you?"

"Japan," Dad said. "I want to find out more about the Samurai warriors—and eat sushi!"

"This is going to be great," said Janie. "Thanks, Mom! Thanks, Dad!"

"I have a challenge for *you* now, Mom," Laura said with a giggle.

Mom raised her eyebrows. "What is it?" she asked.

"We've had so much fun with the

challenges you gave us," Laura explained. "You should give us more challenges for our trip home."

"Yes!" Robbie and Janie agreed.

"And this time, I will be able to join in too!" said Dad.

Chee's Adventure

Joe found himself back in his bedroom, holding *The Book of Neeve*. He looked at the clock. It said 4:15—the exact time he had left.

"What a ride!" said a squeaky voice.

Joe was still wearing his backpack. And Chee was climbing out of it!

"What are you doing here?" Joe asked.

"I want an adventure of my own," said Chee. "You can show me your land, and then I'll return to Neeve through your book."

"Deal!" said Joe happily. "But you'd better hide in the backpack."

Chee scrambled back into his hiding place and Joe went downstairs. "Just going out for a walk, Mom!" he called.

Joe showed Chee the park, the stores and his school.

"I wish I could go to school," said Chee. "It sounds like fun!"

Pear Tree
Elementary

"Better get back home," Joe said. "Mom will have dinner ready soon."

"Thank you for showing me your land, Joe," Chee said, back in Joe's bedroom.

"Ready?" Joe asked him.

"Ready!" Chee replied.

Joe opened *The Book of Neeve* and Chee looked at the picture on the first page. But nothing happened.

"Maybe I can't travel back on my own," Chee suggested.

"Don't worry, I'll take you," said Joe. He looked at the picture, but he didn't even feel dizzy. Joe started flicking through the book. There was some writing he hadn't noticed before.

Use this book with care, for each person may use it only once.

"It looks like I won't be able to get you back," said Joe worriedly. "I'll have to find someone else to do it."

He decided he would ask his best friend, Sarah, to help. "I'll ask her at school tomorrow," he promised Chee.

The next day at school, Joe told Sarah about *The Book of Neeve*. He told her how he'd fallen into a picture and about his adventures with a sprite boy named Chee.

"I don't believe you!" said Sarah.

"Look!" said Joe. He opened his backpack. Chee smiled up at Sarah. He was leaning against *The Book of Neeve*.

"Wow!" Sarah

"Let's take a look," said a voice behind
them. It was Jake, the class bully.
"It's nothing," Joe said.
"Didn't sound like nothing," Jake argued.
He spotted *The Book of Neeve* sticking
out of Joe's backpack and grabbed it.
"Give it back!" Joe shouted. What if
Jake opened the book and looked at
the first page? Just then, the bell rang.
Jake stuffed *The Book of Neeve* into his
backpack. "I'll look at it later," he said,
grinning.

That afternoon, the class went outside to play baseball.

"Joe, you play first base," Coach Jones said and pointed.

Joe had thought about how to get the book back from Jake. He had only come up with one plan. He didn't like it, but it was the best he could do.

"No," Joe said to Coach Jones, rudely.

Coach Jones looked at Joe in surprise.

"You can either play first base, Joe Taylor, or go inside," she said sternly.

Joe hurried back inside, his heart was thumping. He went right to Jake's backpack, took out *The Book of Neeve,* and put it back into his own.

"What do you have to say to me, Joe?" Coach Jones asked, when the class came back in.

"Sorry, Coach," Joe said. "I won't be rude again."

Joe went around to Sarah's house after school with Chee and *The Book of Neeve.*

"Are you sure you want to do this?" he said. "There are goblins and dragons…"

"Of course I am!" said Sarah. "What makes you think that I don't want to have an adventure too?"

"Well… say hello to Mistress Swift and the dragon for me," Joe told her. "And Dolph, Maya, Kala, and Dalin."

"I'll say hello to everyone I see," Sarah said, grinning.

Joe turned to Chee. "Bye, Chee."

"Thanks for a wonderful adventure," Chee smiled. "I wish you could come."

"So do I," said Joe. But secretly he couldn't help thinking he'd had quite enough adventures… for now!

Ice-skating: Lucy's Secret

"Are you coming to the school dance tonight, Lucy?" Sophie asked.

"I can't," Lucy mumbled. She pulled a book from her bag and started to read.

"I don't get it," Sophie said to Daniel after school. "Why doesn't Lucy ever want to join in anything?"

Daniel shook his head. "Maybe she's just shy. Why don't you invite her to our birthday party?"

"I can't," said Sophie. "You know Mom said we can only invite four people each, and I've already invited my four people. What about you?" she asked.

"I've already invited my four people too," Daniel replied.

"We're all going ice skating, right?" Sophie said.

"Right," Daniel said with a grin. "I hope I get the hang of it," he added. "If not, it could end up being a very painful party!"

The day of the party arrived. Daniel, Sophie and their friends wobbled onto the ice. Sophie's ankles turned in and she clutched the rink wall.

CRASH!

She turned toward the sound and then laughed as she saw her brother scrambling around on the ice-covered floor. "Daniel, what are you doing down there?" she joked.

Daniel grabbed the wall and pulled himself up. His skate blades crossed and…*CRASH!* Down he went again. Across the ice, a skater started a slow spin. Sophie watched in awe as the girl  began to twirl faster and faster until she became a blur of gray and black. Then, as the skater brought the spin to a stop, Sophie felt her jaw drop. "Daniel, look!" she said.

Daniel turned to see where Sophie was pointing. "Is that Lucy?" he asked, sounding as surprised as Sophie.

Sophie nodded. They watched as Lucy jumped and twirled. She even skated backward. A man stood nearby calling directions to her.

"Wow!" Daniel said. "She's great!"
The man skated away and Lucy was
alone. Sophie had an idea. She shuffled
across the rink toward Lucy.

"Hi Lucy," she called.

Lucy turned around, surprised. "Oh!
Hi, Sophie," she replied. "What are you
doing here?" She grabbed Sophie's hands
to keep her from falling over.

"Daniel and I have come here for our

birthday," Sophie told her. "But unlike you, we can't skate, we're hopeless. You're an amazing skater!"

Lucy's cheeks went a little pink. "Thanks," she said softly. "My dad taught me. He's my coach."

"You must practice a lot," Sophie said.

Lucy nodded. "I'm in training. Dad keeps me on a strict schedule."

On the other side of the rink there was a shout followed by a thud.

"That must have hurt!" someone said.

Sophie and Lucy looked over to see
Daniel sitting on the ice again. They
laughed. Then there was another shout
from the other side of the rink. This time,
Jason had fallen and was skidding along
the ice on his knees.

"Um, Lucy," Sophie said. "Would you be
able to help us?"

Lucy looked at her skates. "I'd like to,"
she said, "but I'll have to ask my dad."

"Here he comes," Sophie said, seeing
Lucy's father skating toward them.

"Dad, this is Sophie, from school," Lucy told him. "Can I go and help Sophie and the others with their skating?" she asked. "But what about your training?" her dad said with a frown.

There was a pause, then Lucy said, "I love training, Dad. But I want time for friends, too."

Lucy's dad smiled. "OK go on," he agreed. "We can train later."

"Great! Thanks, Dad!" Lucy beamed. She held out her arm to Sophie. "Come on, Sophie, let's skate!"

There's No Such Thing As Magic

Lucy Wilson had sandy-colored hair and freckles. So did her older brother, Mark. Lucy and Mark liked doing the same things, too. They loved jigsaw puzzles and building forts from boxes. But in one way Lucy and Mark were very different. Lucy believed in magic. She believed in spells and magic words.

Mark thought she was crazy. "There's no such thing as magic!" he said. "It's just a load of nonsense. I don't believe in magic."

"You'll change your mind." smiled Lucy.

The next day was Mark's birthday. Along with Mark's cards, the mailman brought a package. Mark's name was on the front.

"It's from Aunt Sadie!" yelled Mark. With a huge smile on his face, Mark ripped open the package. The smile disappeared. "The Box of Tricks—A First Magic Kit," he read out from the lid of the box.

A look of disappointment spread across Mark's face.

Lucy pulled the lid off the box, and took out a folded piece of black cloth.

"A magician's cape!" she gasped. "Look! There's a wand and a bottle of magic dust, too! You can do any magic you want with this."

"Nonsense!" snapped Mark. "There's no such thing as magic!"

The rest of the day was very busy. Mark's friends were coming to dinner, and there was food to prepare, and balloons to blow up. After dinner, when his friends had left, Mark suddenly asked, "Has anyone seen Footsie? I can't remember seeing her all day." Footsie was Mark's cat and he loved her very much.

"Don't worry," said Mom. "She'll be back soon. Maybe all the noise frightened her away."

But Footsie didn't come back.
Even when it grew dark and Dad stood
in the yard calling her name over and
over again, Footsie didn't appear. Next
morning Mark asked Mrs. Kinley next
door if she'd seen Footsie, but she hadn't.
Mark was very worried.

Lucy handed him the magic box.
"We'll just have to do some magic," she
told him. "That'll bring her back."
"Don't be silly, Lucy," said Mark
angrily.
"There's no such thing as magic!"
"Yes, there is!" replied Lucy, throwing
the cloak around herself. She picked up
the magic wand, waved it in the air, and
sang:

"We miss Footsie's quiet purr,
her four white paws and silky fur,
fur that's soft and darkest black,
I wish for Footsie to come back."

"What are you doing?" Mark asked, as Lucy rushed into the kitchen with the small glass bottle. "This will never work."

Lucy didn't listen. She filled Footsie's dish with food and put it by the back door, near the cat flap. Then she sprinkled magic dust all around it.

"You'll see," she said.

Mark woke early the next morning. Lucy

was already in the kitchen. Footsie's bowl was empty, but there was no sign of Footsie.

"How does your special magic dust help now?" sniffed Mark.

"Easy," smiled his sister. "Footsie's been back, hasn't she? And now I know how to find her." She opened the back door and pointed at the pathway. A set of silvery footprints led away from the house.

"Of course!" yelled Mark. "We've just got to follow these." He rushed down the path, following the shiny footprints. They led him down to the back of the shed.

From under the bushes, Mark heard a soft purring noise.

"See!" said Lucy. "I told you magic works. Here's Footsie."

Mark bent down.

"There's no such thing as …" he began. He didn't finish. He turned to Lucy and pulled her down to look. There, under the bushes, lay Footsie and four little kittens.

"Magic!" whispered Mark. Lucy grinned.

The Lion Who Couldn't Roar

Toby the lion cub had a problem. The first time he opened his mouth to roar, all that came out was a squeak! Try as he might, he just couldn't give a lion-like ROAARR! Poor Toby didn't know what to do. Things became even worse when all the other cubs began to laugh at him. "Perhaps I'm not a lion at all," thought

Toby sadly, and wandered off into the jungle. After a while, Toby stopped to rest. Nearby, a small group of mice were playing around under a leafy bush. Toby usually liked to chase mice, but he felt so unhappy, he just couldn't make the effort.

"Look, a lion!" squeaked one mouse. The mice were scared of lions and began to run away.

"I'm not going to hurt you," pleaded Toby. "I'm a mouse too. Listen." Toby opened his mouth and out came a little squeak.

"Can I stay with you, please?" he asked. "I don't have anywhere else to go."

All the mice huddled together, and after a while the biggest mouse said,
"You must be a mouse to squeak like that. We'd be happy for you to stay with us."
So Toby followed the mice into the jungle.
A little while later, the biggest mouse stopped very still, and sniffed the air.
"I smell elephants," he said. "And they're very near."
"What shall we do?" cried the smallest mouse. He was very frightened.

"Run!" yelled the biggest mouse.

Toby and the mice ran off as fast as their legs could carry them. But, since Toby was so much bigger than the mice, he almost trampled them under his feet.

"Be careful, Toby!" shouted the biggest mouse. "You're going to flatten us all!"

Soon they stopped running, and the biggest mouse sniffed the air again.

"All clear," he said. "Let's get some food."

The mice collected all the berries they could find, and put them in a big pile for everyone to share. But Toby thought that the berries were meant for him, and he swallowed them all in one big gulp.

"Mmm, delicious," he said.

"Those berries were meant for all of us," said the biggest mouse, grumpily.

"Sorry!" said Toby.

The mice then collected lots of grass and twigs, which they made into a little house. But, when Toby tried to go inside it, he was far too big to fit in, and the whole thing came crashing down.

"You've destroyed our house, you've eaten all our food and you've almost stepped on us," said the biggest mouse, angrily. "We want you to leave ... now!"

Toby began to walk away slowly, with his tail between his legs. He felt very sad.

"What am I going to do?" he thought.
Just then, he heard a voice behind him.
"Hey, you! Wait a minute!"
It was one of the mice.
"Look!"
You're not a mouse, you're a lion."

"But, I squeak like a mouse," said Toby sadly.

"Don't you worry about that," said Mouse. "I'll help you to get your roar." Mouse jumped into a puddle, and splashed Toby with water.

Toby tried to roar, but all that came out was a squeak. Then Mouse shouted at him. "You're the stupidest lion I've ever seen!" This made Toby angry. He opened his mouth and let out a great big … SQUEAK.

"Hmm," said Mouse.

Mouse decided to go for a refreshing swim in the river. Toby sat at the water's edge, wondering if he'd ever be able to roar. Suddenly, out of the corner of his eye, he noticed a large crocodile

swimming toward Mouse. Toby leaped
to his feet, and tried to warn Mouse,
but all that came out was a squeak! The
crocodile was swimming closer to poor
Mouse.

"This is my final chance," thought Toby.
He opened his mouth again, took a great
big breath, and out came a huge and
terrifying … ROAAAAAAR!!!
When it heard the sound of a roaring lion,
the frightened crocodile swam away.
Mouse swam back. "I told you I'd make
you roar." he said to Toby with a grin.

ROAAAAR!

Toby and Mouse were now great friends.
Toby went back to play with the other
lion cubs. He became a very happy lion,
but he never forgot about the mouse who
taught him to roar.

The Ugly Princess

Princess Cressida lived in a magnificent palace in a faraway land. The princess had no idea that she was very beautiful. Whenever she looked at herself in the mirror, she saw someone who seemed to be extremely ugly.

"How ugly I am!" she would sigh to

herself. "No one has ever looked as ugly as I do."

Princess Cressida's parents, King Otto and Queen Beatrice, were very strict. They knew their daughter was the most beautiful girl in the land, but they didn't want her to know that. The king and queen were worried that their daughter might become very vain. So they took away all the mirrors from the palace, except for one. This mirror was in the princess's bedroom, but it was a trick mirror. So, whenever Princess Cressida looked in the mirror, she saw someone who looked quite ugly.

The princess was a sweet and cheerful girl, so she didn't worry about the way she looked. She was kind and gentle, and everyone who met her loved her.

The king and queen were also strict about where Princess Cressida was allowed to go. So she either stayed in the palace or walked around its huge, wild gardens. Princess Cressida loved to walk through the gardens. Her dog Goldie always came with her, running at the princess's side.

One afternoon, she set off on a walk as usual. "I would so love to be pretty," she said to Goldie, stroking his soft golden head. "But I never will be, so I won't think about it again."

It was a nice day. As the princess walked through the palace grounds, she gazed at the brightly colored flowers. She noticed the beautiful blue sky with hardly a cloud in it, and the pretty birds flying above her. In fact, she was so busy looking at all the beautiful things around her, that she didn't realize she had walked out of the gardens and into the nearby town. While Princess Cressida walked down the street, a crowd of townspeople began to gather around. She noticed they were staring at her. "What's wrong?" she called

out in a trembling voice. But the people said nothing. More people stopped to look at her. Some whispered to each other when they saw her, and two young men bowed as she passed them.

A little further on, another man took off his cloak and laid it on the ground for her to walk on. Princess Cressida was confused and embarrassed.

"Why is everyone behaving like this?" she asked herself. "They are teasing me! I expect they're staring at me because they can't believe that anyone can be so ugly," she sighed.

The princess was almost in tears as she ran away from the crowd into a nearby building. It was dark inside, but she could just make out a room with a small window. Sitting at a table was a young man with his head in his hands. His back was bent in a funny shape, and his clothes were in rags. When the young man raised his head she could see that he was very ugly. He turned away so that the princess could not see his face. "Please don't look at me!" he cried out.

Princess Cressida felt great pity for him. She held out her hand toward him. "Don't hide your face," she said gently. "The way you look means nothing to me."

The young man looked at her. Although his face was ugly, his eyes were kind. "Thank you," said the young man. "No one as beautiful as you has ever spoken so kindly to me before." And he took her outstretched hand in his.

"Me—beautiful?" asked Princess Cressida. She was even more surprised at what happened next. As the young man's hand touched her own, he was instantly changed into a tall and handsome prince.

That was how Princess Cressida learned about her true appearance. She and the prince fell in love at that moment. He told her how a spell had been cast over him at birth, which would only be broken when a beautiful princess was kind to him. At Princess Cressida's wedding, the king and queen asked her to forgive them for their strict behavior. She did. If it hadn't been for her parents, she would never have met her very own Prince Charming!

I Want to Sing

It is not quiet in the jungle. Hidden among the leaves, the jungle friends are calling and talking to each other all day long.

It was a typical noisy morning when Snake had a good idea. He was coiled around a branch, enjoying the warm sunshine. Snake told his idea to a nearby

271

toucan, who was busy cracking nuts. Toucan listened carefully, before tilting her head and blinking her bright eyes. "That's a good idea!" she chirped. "In fact, that's a REALLY GOOD IDEA! I'm going to tell the other animals!" Very soon all the birds and other animals on all the nearby trees knew about Snake's idea. Even Crocodile, who was sliding around in the dark shadows, knew about it. Everyone loved the idea. Snake had suggested starting up a jungle band. Why had no one thought of it before? There would be no

more horrible, loud, screeching noices coming out of the jungle, but the sweet, sweet sound of music instead.

Everyone wanted to be in the band. In a surprisingly short time, the jungle animals had chosen a song and started to rehearse.

The result was amazing. After years of talking away in the noisy jungle all day long, the animals were really good at listening to each other. By noon they sounded as if they had been singing together for years.

"Oooo-oo, oooo-oo!" sang the toucans.
"Snappity, snappity-snap!" went
Crocodile, tapping on a tree stump.
"Hissss, ssss, hissss, ssss!" hissed Snake,
as he wrapped himself around a branch.
"Ee-ee-oo-oo! Ee-ee-oo-oo!" yelled the
monkeys, swinging by their tails in time
to the music.
"That sounds gr-e-e-at!" said Snake.
"One more time!" called toucan.
"A-one, a-two, a-three, four, five …!"

Ooo-oo, ooo-oo! Hisss, ssss, hisss, ssss!
Ee-ee-oo-oo! Ee-ee-oo-oo!
Snappity, snappity-snap!

The song sounded nearly perfect, and
the animals had almost reached the end
when … SQUAAAAAAWK!
"What was that noise?" asked toucan.
"Um … let's do that again," he
suggested. "A-one, a-two, a-three, four,
five …!"

again, they had almost finished the song
when ... SQUAAAAAAWK!
All the animals turned their heads. Not
looking at all embarrassed, sat a parrot.
"Squaaaaawk!" she said cheerfully.
The biggest toucan took charge. "I see
we have a new member of the band. I
wonder if I could ask you to sing a little
more quietly, especially at the end?"
"I thought your song needed a really

BIG finish," replied the parrot. "I can sing it louder, if you like. Listen! SQUAAAAAAAAAWK!"

"NOOO!" cried the toucans and the monkeys and the hummingbirds and Snake and Crocodile.

"Let's try it again," said the biggest toucan. "This time, Parrot, perhaps you could sing in the middle and just ... um ... flap your wings at the end."

The toucan counted them in. "A-one, a-two, a-three, four, five ...!"

Oooo-oo, oooo-oo! Hisss, ssss, hissss, ssss! Squawk, squawk! Ee-ee-oo-oo! Ee-ee-oo-oo! Snappity, snappity-snap! Squaaaawk!

"Sorry!" squawked Parrot. "That noise at the end was me." She had flapped her wings too eagerly and fallen off her perch.

"Let's not have the flapping at the end," suggested the biggest toucan.

"But I want to sing!" cried Parrot.
"Well ... perhaps ... you should flap your wings a little less!" replied the toucan.
"Let's try that one more time. A-one, a-two, a-three, four, five ...!"
It was terrible!
"I got a little carried away at the end," explained Parrot. "I can't help joining in."

Squaaaawk!
Squaaaawk!

"I've got it!" whooped the biggest toucan.
"Every band needs a conductor so why
can't Parrot be OUR conductor? She
knows how to flap her wings!"

"I suppose I could give it a try, if you
think I can do it," replied Parrot.

"You can!" chorused the animals.

"Ready, then ... here goes! A-one, a-five,
a-seven, three, six ...!" called Parrot.

These days, the air is filled with the
beautiful music of the jungle band. And
you only hear a small squawk from a
busy parrot every now and then!

Will the Wizard

Will had six brothers, and they were all older than him. Strangely, Will's dad also had six brothers who were also older than he was. Will's mom said that the seventh son of a seventh son was always a very clever wizard. Mom only said it as a joke, but Will believed her even though he couldn't do magic—and he was

was only six years old. Will was really excited to think that he was a real wizard. He told all his brothers and all his uncles *and* all his friends, but they didn't believe him one bit. They laughed and said, "Of course you are!"
Each Tuesday afternoon at school, Will's class studied drawing and

painting. One Tuesday, Wills made a tall pointy hat out of black construction paper. He glued on lots of shiny stars, and added a bolt of lightning in silver foil, too.

Next, he made a wand from a stick and another shiny star. It was great! It looked as if it would really work—as if powerful magic was bottled up inside, itching to get out and do something amazing.

Will practiced waving his wand—he didn't want magic to happen accidentally because he hadn't waved it correctly.

Will's friends teased him, asking him when they could see some real magic.

Will knew they didn't believe he was a wizard. He did think, for a minute, of turning his best friend John into a frog, just to see the look on his friends' faces. But no, that was not how a wizard should behave. And yet, it wouldn't do any harm to practice turning things into frogs, would it?

Will and his friends looked around for something that no one would miss. They found an old bucket. Will gracefully passed his wand over the bucket. "Abracadabra!" he cried. It was the only magic word he knew—but the bucket did not change. His friends laughed. Will's friends laughed again when he tried to turn a traffic cone into a giant ice cream, and a tree trunk into chocolate pudding. Will began to feel disappointed. The next day Ms. Green, Will's teacher, took the whole class out to the nearby park. Will had left his pointy hat and wand behind.

He was fed up with everyone laughing at him. People who were not wizards just didn't understand.

When the children had been in the park for a while, they heard a loud crackling sound and smelled smoke. It was a forest fire! The children could see fierce flames blowing toward some houses at the edge of the park.

"Oh no!" cried Will's friend John. "My house is over there! It'll be burned to the ground!" Then Ms. Green said that her house was nearby too, just where the flames were blowing. She gathered up the children and led them away from any

danger, but she was really worried about her house. "What a shame I don't have my wand!" Will said to John, who was walking along next to him. "I could have pointed it like this," Wills pointed a finger up at the sky. "And I could have said, um ... CHICKEN NUGGETS AND POPCORN!"

As he said these words, a huge bolt of lightning flew from Will's finger up into the sky. The thunder was so loud that it knocked everyone off their feet. Finally, the thunder grew quieter and quieter, until it fizzled out altogether. Will looked at his finger in amazement, then a huge smile spread slowly over his face.

"Or I could just point my finger like this," he said, "and say PEANUT BUTTER AND FRENCH FRIES! This time the lightning bolt was even brighter, and the thunder even louder. Then Will used both hands and yelled anything that came into his head.

There was a huge bolt of lightning in the sky, followed by a large rumble of

thunder. The sky darkened and soon rain was pouring down, but only where the fire was burning. Where the children stood it was still dry and sunny. Everyone was cheering Will—they were truly amazed at his magic.

Will had put out the fire and saved the houses. He hadn't needed his hat and wand after all, nor his magic words. The magic power was all in him ... Will. Will, the hero.

WILL ... THE WIZARD!